THE H

OF BLACK AFRICA

By

STEVEN S. JACOBS

PART II OF THIS BOOK BY
MOSES FARRAR

DEDICATIONS

To the innumerable millions stolen away from
Western and Southern Africa by Europeans,
from 1517 to 1808, and sold into slavery
in the Western Hemisphere . . .

To the untold millions of men, women and children
who perished in the Middle Passage . . .

To all the Africans and their descendants who were victims
of the Slave Trade and who served as slaves in the
Western World for 348 years . . .

To all the Africans and their descendants who were
lynched, raped, flogged, flayed, etc., during the
abominable days of Slavery . . .

To everyone of all races and nationalities who championed
and are still championing the cause of freedom for
oppressed peoples throughout the world.

TABLE OF CONTENTS

PART II

FOREWORD

STEPHEN S. JACOBS, a European Jew, has, beyond the shadow of a doubt, fully documented in this book, THE HEBREW HERITAGE OF BLACK AFRICA, that the Hebrews/Israelites/Jews of Biblical times were of the Black race and lived on the African and Asian (Middle East region) continents of the world.

In tracing the journeyings of the ancient Hebrew Israelites from Jerusalem to Assyria to Babylon and throughout the length and breadth of Africa -- and particularly to the shores of West Africa where the Slave Trade began -- Jacobs brings to light facts which mainstream electronic and print media have chosen to ignore and even silence. His research is thorough and precise, contains quotations from many anthropologists, historians and professors, and is complete with photographs, seven pages of bibliography, maps and illustrations.

This book is a must-read for people of all races and belief systems, for it satisfies the need to dispel the lies which have enveloped the minds of the masses into believing that the White European Jews are the original *"people of the Book"* and the chosen people of God expressed throughout the Bible. More and more White Jews (especially the older ones) are acknowledging in secret to those of us who already know, that *"the original Jews were Black."* Scores of authors, Black and White, have now written extensively over the last fifty or more years on the subject of the presence of Black Hebrew Israelites not only on the continents of Africa and Asia but on other continents, as well. Some of these Hebraic people are descendants of the <u>originals,</u> and thousands more have <u>returned</u> to the worship of the Almighty God of their forefathers, the God of Abraham, the God of Isaac, and the God of Jacob, after having been forced in time past to embrace other religions through foreign colonization.

It is hoped that after reading this and other books on the subject, millions more of African ancestry will not only <u>agree</u> with the contents, but will also make an informed decision to <u>reclaim</u> and <u>practice</u> the way of life ordained by the Creator through His holy prophets. The Most High is working His will through preachers, teachers and authors to bring back His people who have gone astray, saying to them, *"Return unto Me; for I have redeemed thee"* (Isaiah 44:22).

Part II of This Book

MOSES FARRAR, author of *THE DECEIVING OF THE BLACK RACE* and *A NON-CHRISTIAN'S RESPONSE TO CHRISTIANITY*, is writer of the second portion of this book. In this section I enter into a discussion on the head patriarch of the Israelites, Abraham, entitled "ABRAHAM, THE FRIEND OF GOD." He is the one to whom three of the major religions of the world -- Judaic, Christian, and Islamic -- express fealty.

Part II also contains, but is not limited to, the following topics:

"FROM ABRAHAM TO DAVID TO JESUS"; a poem entitled "THE BIBLE: HOW READEST THOU?"; A NIGERIAN FOLK TALE; lots of *"here a little and there a little"* nuggets of knowledge, and other food for the soul and mind. (See table of contents for complete listing.)

You are going to love this section, too -- I guarantee it!

HAPPY READING!

AUTHOR'S MOTTO: *"I will proclaim and publish the NAME of the LORD GOD ALMIGHTY, and ascribe greatness unto Him."*

vi

שְׁמַע יִשְׂרָאֵל, יְיָ אֱלֹהֵינוּ, יְיָ ׀ אֶחָד:

Sh'ma, Yisrael, Adonai Elohénu Adonai Echod.

Hear, O Israel, the LORD is our God, the LORD is one.

Chapter One

THE IMPORTANCE OF THIS BOOK

ARE AFRICAN AMERICANS the descendants of the ancient Hebrews of the Middle East?

This question is answered in the affirmative, with a resounding yes, by Professor Joseph J. Williams after more than eleven years of intensive research into the subject. In his book entitled HEBREWISMS OF WEST AFRICA, this eminent scholar documents the origins and the extent of Hebrew culture and religion in that part of West Africa, along the Atlantic bulge of the continent, which is the ancestral home of most African Americans. He goes farther than simply documenting the influences of the Hebrews in West Africa, he concludes that the ancient Hebrews are "parent stock" from which present-day Black American peoples actually evolved.[1]

For those who are unacquainted with the late Professor Williams, his scholarly credentials are beyond dispute. Beside devoting over eleven years of active research into this subject, he held a doctoral degree in Cultural Anthropology. He was a fellow (member) of the British Royal Geographical Society and its American counterpart, the American Geographical Society. He was a member of the International Institute of African Languages and Cultures. He belonged to the Catholic Anthropological Conference, and was on the faculty of the noted Jesuit institution of higher learning, Boston College. And not the least, he was a linguist and the author of several books, papers and articles on the subjects of Black

9

civilization and culture in Africa and the West Indies.

The scholarship of Professor Williams, as well as many other scholars and eye-witnesses, is collected, digested, updated and supplemented in this new volume called THE HEBREW HERITAGE OF BLACK AFRICA. The purpose of writing this book is to bring to its readers and to the public at large, whether lay person or scholar, an insight into and perspective of the Black heritage with which they previously may have been unaware.

The truth is that this book is meant to provide more than cold, hard facts or historical insights, as important as each is. The book has a spiritual dimension as well. It is the hope of your author that reading it will stimulate pride and sense of destiny on the part of Black and Brown people everywhere. This comes with knowing who you are, where you came from, and where you ought to be heading. And this book is for the consumption of people of other skin colors who want to learn more about and to better understand their darker skinned friends and neighbors.

In this age when the Black person is striving as never before in modern history to learn more about himself and his origins, this book is intended as a source for such information. To Black Jews and White Jews alike, it should provide further evidence of the universality of their faith and the culture for which it serves as cornerstone. And to everyone, regardless of color or belief, this book should reveal that Black culture, far from being lost in the backwaters of the African jungle, was and continues to be very much in the mainstream of history.

Additionally, this book is written at a time when Black peoples the world over are seeking to rediscover their own identities. Not satisfied to learn only about White European history and its heroes, Black people in their intellectual and spiritual reawakening want and in fact deserve to know who they are. Only in this way can they decide for themselves in freedom who they are and want to be. The whole person, after all, is a product of his or her past and present, even though the details of the former are hidden by the mists of time. No one can totally escape his heritage any more than he can escape the world in which he was born and presently lives. Both past and present exist in each of us. It is reflected by our customs, our habits, our attitudes and those of others toward us, by our physical appearance, the people with whom we associate and identify, and in many other ways.

It is very important at the outset of this book to recognize that no one, no religion, no culture, nor any other institution of life was created or exists on a vacuum. In a very real sense, all men and women are brothers and sisters. We are part of a continuation of the same two dimensions of time and space. We are, in short, part of the same world, whether we like it or not. We come from societies and cultures which are inter-related and intertwined both in the past and present. In truth, nothing is completely pure or isolated, whether we talk in terms of race or religion or politics or society or any other aspect or discipline in life. This is just as true of those who live in Africa as for those who live in Europe or Asia or anywhere else.

What, for example, is generally thought to be distinctively Jewish by persons of European ancestry is far different from what is considered Jewish by people of Asian or African descent. Bagels and lox (donut-shaped rolls and salmon) are considered "native" to most European Jews. In fact, these foods are Slavic and not Hebrew in origin. The common language of Central and East European Jews, called Yiddish, really is Eleventh Century German with an admixture of Slavic and Hebrew words and expressions. The very word "synagogue," which has become associated with the Jewish house of prayer, actually is a Greek word. Even the word

"Jew" came into popular usage after the words "Hebrew" and "Israelite," the former ("Jew") originally applying only to those who were of the tribe of Judah which at one time was only part of the larger Israelite nation. In fact, it is for this last-mentioned reason that most Black Jews prefer to refer to themselves as "Israelites" or "Hebrew Israelites" to distinguish themselves from their White Jewish counterparts.

In the same way that European Jewish customs and practices contain much that is not pure in origin, the same can be said about the Hebraic civilization of Black Africa. The fact is that the Hebrew influences in both Europe and Africa, as well as in Asia, have been diluted with the passage of time. Our purpose, however, is not to stress the differences which have arisen from the processes of history, but rather it is to find those elements which bind people together.

What, then, can be offered as evidence of a Hebraic background among the peoples of and from Black Africa, particularly that part of the continent -- West Africa -- from whence most of the New World slaves came? The answer is given to us by Professor Williams and the others who speak to us through the pages of this book. Their research, their findings, and their eye-witness experiences prove once and for all that Judaism [or the way of life that has come to be so called by some], the culture and religion of the Hebrews, is rooted deeply in the native soil of Black Africa. What we will discover is not merely that the history of Black Africa is tied to that of the Middle East, but also that Black people and Hebrew civilization were synonymous from the time of the Hebrew patriarch Abraham onwards, in Africa and in the Middle East itself.

Although Professor Williams deals with the evidence of Hebrew culture in Africa and the Caribbean, he nonetheless alludes to the existence of "Black Jews" in the Middle East when he quotes Sir Harry Johnston, the leading British authority on Black anthropology in the nineteenth century, that "negroid people with kinky hair" inhabited the Babylonian homeland of the patriarch Abraham.[2] For those who are not familiar, ancient Babylonia today is called Iraq, very much a Middle Eastern nation. Williams says this conclusion makes it easier to show "the same Hebrew stock in the evolving of certain tribes in Africa."[3] Just how correct Williams is to rely on the scholarly conclusions reached by Johnston, we shall shortly see.

The first part of our book deals largely with Black West African history and culture. We do this step by step. Once we establish the existence and importance of Hebrew civilization and culture there, we move to other parts of Black Africa and then to the Middle East. Finally, we shift our attention to America and modern times. To fully update our book and to modernize some of the more archaic wording and grammar of our older sources, some of which date back several centuries, and to make your reading a bit easier, we occasionally make grammatical changes and add editorial notes and comments of our own. We attempt, no matter, to remain faithful to the actual meanings and impressions of the scholars and eye-witnesses we record.

Chapter Two

THE BROADER SCENE

BEFORE WE SET FOOT upon the distant shores of Africa and the Middle East, we want to remind you that the pages which follow actually represent the thoughts, observations, knowledge and conclusions of many scholars and eye-witnesses. We merely are the editors in a sense of what already has been uncovered and written about, albeit not widely known by the public. In another sense we have put together pieces of a jigsaw puzzle. The pieces have been here, almost in front of our eyes. What has been needed is for someone to put them into their proper places.

There is a well-known expression that "A rose is a rose by any other name!" This means simply that a rose is a rose, no matter what else it might be called. We who live in America are accustomed to thinking in terms of European language and culture. This applies to Black people as well as White. "Negro" is a word of Spanish derivation; "colored" and "black" are English words. Rarely does the Black man think of himself as a descendant of the Ashanti, Fanti, Yoruba or other West African ethnic groups. Yet he remains a person with the same heritage, the same historical experiences and background, and the same kindred feelings and emotions as most others of Black African descent.

In this same sense, such a person has a Black Israelite heritage, whether he uses this term or not, or whether he knows it or not. Because these words are not customarily used by most Black Americans does not mean they do not apply. We in America tend to associate the word "Jew" and

14

"Hebrew" with White people because of our European cultural conditioning. A trip to the State of Israel would dispel this notion immediately. There you will find Jews of all colors and ethnic backgrounds living side by side. And historically we can read in our own history books on African history that Black Africans, e.g. the Falasha of Ethiopia, were Jews long before Christianity or Islam made an appearance on the scene.

It must be kept in mind that the Black man did not have control of his own destiny until recently. He was obliged and conditioned to accept the norms of others, and slavery and near-slavery have been the rule in the United States. The ravages of inter-tribal warfare over the centuries and the intrusion of colonial and alien missionary forces combined to all but obliterate the knowledge of the distant past among the Africans themselves. Even where and when the Black man finally gained his freedom, he remained culturally castrated. He lacked the tools, as any sociologist would agree, to be master of his own house. These tools include a homogeneous family and community life, an unbroken tradition of education and cultural self-awareness, political and economic independence, and the psychological self-assurance that comes with being a genuine first-class citizen.

The White man, as is logical of human nature, has written and interpreted history largely from his own point of view. Take the following illustration as an example: Not long ago the capital city of the Republic of Zaire (formerly the Belgian Congo) was featured in an article in a prominent American newspaper. It was written by a White man. The article mentioned the "native quarter" of Kinshasha, referring to the section where its black citizens live. Here lies the rub!: The description of Black people living in a native quarter is grossly misleading. The word "quarter" implies something much less than the whole. It would appear to the ordinary reader whose mind retains the superficial impressions of his reading, that the native Black Africans therefore live in a relatively small section of the city. The fact is that nearly everyone in Kinshasha is Black as they are in the country as a whole. To speak of a "black quarter" there is to suggest the existence of a black minority. Nothing is farther from the truth!

The history of Israel has been handed down to us mostly from White scholars. As a result, the emphasis has been put on what ties Europe and Europeans to the Middle East. The possibility of a relationship between Black Africa and the Middle East is rarely mentioned.

The bias in our knowledge of history runs deep. It is reflected, for example, by the fact that little space is devoted to the historic and theological kinship between Christianity and the so-called pagan Greco-Roman religions of 2,000 years ago. It also is reflected by the fact that relatively few books deal with the non-Hebraic ancestry of most White Jews who are descendants of Greeks, Romans, Armenians, Berbers and others who adopted or converted to Judaism during the period of its greatest expansion in the Mediterranean area before the Christian era began. Certainly, few White historians are able to plumb the depths of anguish and despair suffered by Black Africans who, like cattle, once were herded to the Western Hemisphere as slaves.

No single book can deal exhaustively with any subject so that every facet and opinion is recorded therein. Our book is no exception. It is not written to rehash old viewpoints and biases. It is not to rewrite of White history in Europe or the Middle East. Our purpose among others is to redress what we believe is a long-standing imbalance in the presentation of Black history. We want to introduce you and every reader to a part of Black history which cannot be found in the standard texts and treatises on the subject. Black Americans now are in position as never before in modern history to rediscover, and reclaim if they wish, a heritage which has profoundly influenced world history and mankind: the Hebrew heritage of Black Africa.

Chapter Three

THE ASHANTI OF WEST AFRICA

PROFESSOR JOSEPH WILLIAMS begins his book, *Hebrewisms of West Africa,* by recalling his discoveries and observations while livng on the West Indies island of Jamaica. Intrigued by certain similarities between Jamaican customs and those of Ancient Hebrews, this famous Jesuit scholar began an eleven-year search to determine if there really were affinities between Middle East customs and those found in Black Africa and the West Indies.

The following are the words of Dr. Williams which summarize his reasons for pursuing the subject. He says that "to understand properly the spirit and aspirations of the Jamaican peasant, a close study of the (African) Ashanti* themselves became necessary." And this study in turn led him to some rather startling results and conclusions.

"In the first place," he continues, "many Hebrewisms were discovered in Ashanti tribal customs. Then several Ashanti words were found to have a striking resemblance to those of evuivalent Hebrew meaming. Finally, the Supreme Being of the Ashanti gave strong evidence of being the Yahweh (God) of the Old Testament.

"The question," he asks, "naturally arose, how to explain these parallel cultural traits? Should they be ascribed to mere coincidence or to independent development? Or have we here a remarkable instance of diffusion across the entire breadth of (Black) Africa? Is it possible to establish even a partial historical contact between the Ashanti of today and the

*pronounced: a-SHÄN-tee

18

Hebrews of fully two thousand years ago or more?"[1]

It is to the Ashanti that Professor Williams devotes much of his research. The reasons why he did this are several. The Ashanti are a relatively large grouping of people, not just an isolated tribe. They and related groups of people live in an area roughly the same as where the slave ancestors of most Black Americans came. This is confirmed by Daniel Mannix and Malcom Cowley in their best-selling book, *Black Cargoes: A History of the Atlantic Slave Trade*, written in 1962. They say, "Most of the New World's slaves came from tribes living within 200 miles of the (Atlantic) coast. A disproportionate share of them belonged to the Ashanti-speaking, Yoruba-speaking, or Ewe-speaking peoples living in what are now Ghana, Dahomey and Nigeria."[2]

Today this region is divided into several independent nations. They include the three mentioned in the paragraph above as well as the republics of Gambia, Senegal, Guinea, Ivory Coast, Togo, and Cameroon. The boundaries of these countries were established almost arbitrarily prior to their independence as a result of the military conquests and political intrigues and compromises of the European colonial rulers. For these reasons every tribal grouping of any consequence can be found to overlap national borders as they exist today.

The result is that the Ashanti are found in a wide area of West Africa, not merely inside the boundaries of present-day Ghana. In fact, they are sufficiently numerous that particularly every other contiguous tribal grouping is in some way interrelated. According to Ernest Chantre, former Director of the Anthropological Society of Lyons, France, "The Ashanti do not constitute a pure ethnic group but an aggregate of negro types."[3]

The problem confronting Professor Williams was whether the lineage of these Ashanti could be traced or connected to other earlier civilizations. André Arcin, a noted historian at the turn of the nineteenth century, is quoted by Williams to conclude that "from Ethiopia, Middle Egypt and Central Sudan descended the Ashanti and the tribes known as Bantu."[4] In short, Arcin and Williams conclude that the Ashanti had migrated to the West Coast of Africa from the eastern side of the same continent.

Professor Roland B. Dixon, an anthropologist from Harvard University, in his study of the physical characteristics of the Ashanti, notes a similarity "to the Chad group of people in the Sudan."[5] The Sudanese Republic is in the northeastern section of African, near Egypt and Ethiopia. "The Black immigration," he adds, "was in part a direct southward movement from the western Sudan and the Sahara borders forced by the expansion in the Sahara region of the Caucasian (White) peoples who poured into northern Africa since very early times."[6]

Dr. Hermann Bauman, a Curator at the State Museum of Anthropology in Berlin, West Germany, concludes that the Ashanti are to be classified with "the strongly Sudanese, Yoruba and Nupe."[7] The historian, Walter Claridge, in his book about the history of Ghana and the Ashanti, says, "The Fani, Ashantis, Wassawa, and in fact all the Twi-speaking or Akan peoples were originally one tribe."[8]

In summary, we find the following general observations are made by several scholars mentioned above:

1. The Ashanti are an ethnic mixture of the peoples of West Africa, the ancestral home of most Black Americans.
2. The Ashanti are closely related to the Fanti, Yoruba, Sudanese, and more distantly to the Bantu, whose combined population stretches fully across sub-Saharan Africa.
3. The Ashanti tribes appear to have migrated and later been pushed westward and southward by alien White

invaders of European origin now known as Berbers and Arabs. The Ashanti appear to have spread from the Chad-Nile region of Northeast Africa.

4. The Ashanti and related peoples live in the very region near the West Coast of Africa from which most Black African slaves were captured and transported. Hence they are the ancestors of most African Americans of today.

But the question still remains, as the title of our book implies, whether the earlier Ashanti and related peoples have any connection with the Hebrews of the Middle East. The answer which Professor Williams reaches is that the similarities are too great to ignore and can be accounted for only by the fact that the ancient Hebrews are "parent stock from which the present Ashanti evolved."[9] In fact, it was the "continuous influx of Hebrew settlers trekking up the Nile" which he says "eventually spread itself clear across Africa to the Niger (river) and thence pretty much the whole of West Africa."[10]

There is no doubt in the mind of Professor Williams that the Ashanti are part of the blood and culture of earlier Hebrews who migrated from the Middle East. Nor is there any doubt that these same Ashantis are related today to nearly every tribal grouping in Black West Africa. The evidence according to Professor Williams is cumulative and revealed by the many striking similarities between the civilizations of Black West Africa and the Hebrew Middle East. And it is reinforced, as we shall see, by similar parallels throughout the rest of Black Africa, as well.

Chapter Four

ASHANTI HEBREWISMS

THE PREVIOUS CHAPTERS were designed to set the scene for what follows and to acclimatize us to our goals and purposes -- the search for the Hebrew heritage of Black Africa. What we are looking for is not so much the oyster shells which are littered about on the ocean floor, but the occasional pearls inside. Our aim is to uncover those facets of culture and religion which historically underlie the fabric of Black African life. This particular chapter helps us open the shell. The basic elements for which we are looking are discussed in those chapters that follow this one.

This chapter is devoted to an analysis of some of the similarities between Ashanti and Hebrew customs and practices in two basic categories: language usage, and customs and religious practices. The study reveals striking similarities. It also uncovers factors which appear unrelated at first glance but are very much alike upon closer examination.

Professor R. Sutherland Rattray, in his book *RELIGION AND ART IN ASHANTI*, says the Ashanti word *obayifo* means 'female witch' or 'sorceress.'[1] According to J. G. Christaller, in his famous dictionary of the Ashanti language, still considered one of the most exhaustive of its kind, this word is derived from *obayen* which in turn is a compound of *ob* and *ayen* which he says mean 'witch-wizard' or 'soothsayer' when put together.[2] This compound word, whose West Indian (Jamaican) equivalent is *obeah,* can be traced "to the Canaanite superstition of *Ob*," says another linguistics expert, John

Bathurst Dean, in his 1833 book entitled *THE WORSHIP OF THE SERVANT*.[3]

M. Oldfield Howey, a noted expert on African culture, notes more pointedly that "the witch of Endor is spoken of as an _ob_ and was applied to be King Saul as an oracle" or fortune-teller.   In his book, *THE ENCIRCLED SERPENT*, he explains that "today among some Blacks the same is found. The ob-man or ob-woman is habitually consulted in any case of doubt and difficulty, just as was the ob-woman of Endor by King Saul."[4]   His reference is to the witch of Endor, a village in the Gallilee area of Israel, who the Bible in I Samuel 28:8-25 says was visited by King Saul some 3,000 years ago before his last battle with the Philistines.

Williams observes that "the very term used by the native, to 'make _ob,_' which has come to Jamaica from the old Ashanti slaves, is idiomatically the same as the Scriptural _C'Asa Ob_ found in II Kinds 21:6 of the Bible, one of the crimes charged against King Manasseh, and which literally means '*he made ob.*'"[5]

"The very word _Ashanti_ has itself a strong Hebraic flavor," says Williams.   "The terminal syllable 'ti' in the names of West African tribes usually has the general meaning of 'the race of' or 'the men of' or 'the children of,'" explains Louis Desplagnes in his book about the central plateau region of Nigeria.[6]   Williams reaches the same conclusion that "this would make Ashanti 'the people of Ashan.'   There was, in fact, a town of the name Ashan in the domain of Judah."[7]

Dr. Gerson B. Levi talks about Ashan in his contribution of the same name in the world-famous *JEWISH ENCYCLOPEDIA*. He fully supports the views of Professor Williams because he says "Ashan: Town in the domain of Judah (Joshua 15:42), but which was in the actual possession of Simeon (Joshua 19:7; I Chronicles 4:32)."[8]

"The primary meaning of the Hebrew word 'Ashan' is

'smoke'," comments Williams, "and it is used mainly to describe a burning city, and secondly (as) the figurative destruction of Israel." [9] He cites the HEBREW AND ENGLISH LEXICON of Brown, Driver and Briggs as his source for this conclusion. "The latter meaning," he continues, "would be significant and certainly applicable to fugitives from Jerusalem." [10]

Even the word _Amen_ appears in both the Ashanti and Hebrew languages. Professor R. Sutherland Rattray in his ASHANTI PROVERBS cites an old Ashanti hymn of thanks to the Supreme Being (God) in which the word appears. According to this renowned ethnologist, the use of the word by the Ashanti predated the arrival of Christian missionaries in West Africa. [11]

The study of general Ashanti and Hebrew grammars also reveals other similarities which cannot be summarily dismissed. J. G. Christaller explains, for example, that the relative participle in the Ashanti language "serves to make up for the lack of relative pronouns, just as in Hebrew." [12] In addition, the negative in Ashanti usually is formed by the prefix _n_ which means "not." [13] The noun-clause in Hebrew likewise is made negative by the adverb _en_ which literally means "it is not." [14]

Williams remarks that "a careful study of Professor Rattray's ASHANTI PROVERBS discloses many indications of seeming Hebrew affinity or rather influence." [15] Moreover, he observes "the parallelism so distinctive of Hebrew poetry also found in the Ashanti." [16] By this he has reference to the repeating of words and phrases for the purpose of emphasis. It is found throughout the Bible and elsewhere in Hebrew literature.

Although the examples given above are scattered illustrations, they non-the-less give us some clues that we are headed in the right direction. We can begin to apply these grammatic clues by examining some of the Ashanti and Hebrew cultural and religious characteristics which they appear to have in common. We separate the words "culture" and "religion" for the sake of emphasis; however, it should be recognized that the latter actually is a part of the former. In the case of agrarian societies of the past, there was no full separation of church and state as has evolved in modern society. We deal below with a few examples of cultural and religious similarities which represented important occasions in the lives of the peoples about whom we are concerned.

According to Professor Williams, the Mosaic laws concerning marriages within the Israelite tribes were designed to preserve the inheritance of the daughters within the fanily of their fathers, such as those described in Numbers 36:5-12, are very similar to Ashanti customs.[17] And, he says, the cross-cousin marriages of the Ashanti[18] "are strictly similar to that of the Hebrew daughters of Salphaas who . . . wed 'the sons of the brothers of their fathers (Numbers 36:11).' "[19] If these laws seem outmoded today, it must be remembered in perspective that they were very important in those ancient days and in more primitive societies where family ties and land inheritance played important roles in marriage.

The Ashanti marriage customs, says Rattray, require that the prospective bride and groom first satisfy each other that their marriage will not violate the tribal laws about marriage between blood relatives. These are called laws of consangruinity. Then, after getting the consent of the parents of the bride, the groom offers a dowery and a wine offering. After the wine is passed to those present at the wedding, what remains of it is poured on the ground. These are the only requirements; no priest is even needed.[20]

Professor Williams observes by comparison that "in the ancient Hebrew marriage, the ceremony was performed in a private house without the necessary presence of a priest or rabbi. An elder invoked the benediction and gave a cup of wine to the bride and groom who pledged fidelity to each other. The bridegroom then dashed the cup to the ground. The marriage contract was then read and attested by the drinking of a cup of wine by each person present "almost exactly as do the Ashanti."[21]

One of the interesting similarities between Ashanti and ancient Hebrew customs is in the realm of child-birth practices. For example, the Ashanti mother is considered "unclean" for eight days after the birth of her child. On the eighth day the child is given a name and on the fortieth day a related ceremony is observed.[22] "In all this we certainly are reminded of Hebrew customs, " says Williams -- and correctly so. Even the restrictions and taboos of the Ashanti woman during her menstrual period, including her seclusion, "read like a page borrowed from the book of Leviticus," he says with obvious reference to the twelfth chapter.[23]

In summary, we safely can say that the Ashanti language contains much that closely resembles ancient Hebrew, including the word Ashanti itself. We also find the two cultures have important customs in common. Add to these the certainty that the Ashanti migrated from the general direction of the Middle East and we can perceive a close link between the two peoples, if not a common ancestry. Just how close this link is, we can more fully judge by reading the next chapters.

Chapter Five

THE SUPREME BEING
OF THE ASHANTI

MOST PEOPLE WHO LIVE outside of Black Africa, and even those inside who have been Christianized or Islamized, think of the indigenous African religions as polytheistic and idolatrous. If asked to find similarities between native Black African and Hebrew concepts of God, for instance, the likely answer is that there are none. After all, most people reason that native African religions have many gods; Jews believe in only one.

Here is a perfect example of how long-standing historical biases create unbalanced pictures of what people believe. A closer examination of African religious beliefs reveals the nature and extent of this bias.

It first is helpful to make ourselves aware of the actual condition of Hebrew religious beliefs and practices during the Biblical era to make a proper comparison between Black African and Hebrew religion. Professor George Foot Moore, a Harvard University historian, states that "the Biblical forefathers had fallen away from the true religion, not only by worshipping other gods, but by worshipping their own God in a heathen way." [1] Dr. A. W. Blunt, a well-known archeologist, notes that "to a late date, as excavations prove, the Israelites continued to use models of cows and plagues of Ashtoreth as amulets." [2] Ashtoreth was the ancient Semitic goddess of fertility with counterparts among the Greeks, Romans and

Egyptians.

Another historian, R. L. Ottley, confirms the views expressed above. He says, "The Hebrews did not openly abandon their allegiance to Yehovah, but they co-ordinated and sometimes even identified their national Deity with one or other of the Canaanite gods. Thus the simple and pure worship of Yehovah gradually was corrupted by the admixtures of usages and symbols borrowed from the nature worship of the Canaanites."[3]

Illustrations of this situation abound in the Bible. For example, Chapter 23 of II Kings lists several examples, including the fact that King Solomon himself built altars to Ashtoreth. None-the-less, F. Pret, in his article in the _Dictionnaire de la Bible_, observes that "the idolatry of the Hebrews (during that era) was less an apostasy than the adoption of strange practices and ceremonies."[4]

Thus we can see, almost at a glance, a certain parallel between the historical condition of Biblical Israel and that commonly attributed to Black African religions. The awareness that ancient Israel also suffered many corruptions in its religious practices and beliefs should make us more tolerant and help remove some of the mental obstacles in our investigations of the similarities between the two traditions.

We might look to start at the conclusions of William Bosman. He wrote several books in the early 18th Century about his first-hand experiences with the peoples of the Gold Coast of West Africa. This is the area we know today as Ghana, Togo and Dahomey. He notes in no uncertain words that these people "ascribe to God the attributes of Omnipresence, Omniscience and Invisibility, besides which they believe He governs all things by Providence. By reason God is invisible, they say it would be absurd to make any human representation of Him" (as do Christians). For this reason, he says, the idols before which they worship only represent at best "subordinate deities."[5]

At this juncture it might be well to consider whether the African concept of the Almighty God stems from Christian or Islamic influences. Professor Rattray, whom Williams calls "a master of the Ashanti language and an official interpreter in several other dialects," asserts "I am convinced that the Ashanti conception of a Supreme Being has nothing whatever to do with Christian missionary influence or Islam (Muslims)."[6] He adds, "In a sense it is true that this great Supreme Being, the concept of which is inately Ashanti, is the Jehovah of the Israelites."[7]

The views which we have recorded and discussed thus far largely are of a general nature. In this very important area of theology the question naturally arises whether there are specific proofs that the Almighty God of the Ashanti and that of the Hebrews are one and the same. We think the following evidence that they are should satisfy all but the incredulous!

First let us compare the Ashanti and Hebrew names for God. The full name of the Supreme Being or God of the Ashanti is _onyame_. The _o_ ordinarily is not pronounced, so the spelling _nyame_ is more exact phonetically. The _n_ is a prefix to convey the idea of immensity. This leaves the root word _yame_.[8] Rattray and Christaller, whom we mentioned before as experts in the Ashanti language, both agree that the letter _m_ is interchangeable with _w_ in the Ashanti language.[9] In other words, the Ashanti name for God can be pronounced _Yame_ or _Yawe_, the vowels basically being short.

Although the pronunciation of the vowels is somewhat variable in Biblical Hebrew because the word Yahweh originally was a totally consonantal word -- a word without vowels -- the situation nevertheless is almost identical with the Ashanti usage. Dr. Albert T. Clay, an archeologist and linguistics expert at Yale University, notes in his THE EMPIRE OF THE AMORITES, that "In the Murushu archives found at Nippur during the reigns of Artaxerxes and Darius (in Persia), the divine element in Hebrew names is written *Ja-a-ma* for *Yawa*." He also mentions a clay tablet found at Ta'anach which "contains the divine name of Israel's God written as *Jami*." [10] He concludes unhesitatingly that "some Semitic groups used *m* and others *w* to represent the same sound." [11] Thus we learn from separate and independent sources that the word for Almighty God may be spelled or pronounced as *Yawe* or *Yame* in both Hebrew and Ashanti.

However, the similarity does not end here. The word for the divine Creator in Ashanti is *Bore-bore*.[12] The exact Hebrew equivalent in sound and meaning is *Bore*.[13] This is the participle form for the Hebrew word meaning "to create."[14] The word *bore* [created], for example, is found in Isaiah 42:5 of the Bible.

In the Ashanti language, God also is called *Nyankapon Kwame*, which means "God alone, Great One, to whom Sabbath [Saturday] is dedicated." This dedication to the Sabbath of the Almighty is verified in a letter written in 1922 by the last Ashanti queen, Amma Sewa Akota, to the wife of the then British governor of the Gold Coast. The letter contains the passage "The great God Nyankopon . . . whose day of worship is a Saturday."[15] Once again we have another similarity to a very important Hebrew concept, the observance of Saturday as the Sabbath in memory of the Creation by Almighty God (Genesis 2:1-3).

Certain Christian theologians have sought to liken the visualization of the Ashanti Supreme Being with the popular notion of the Christians that God also is represented in human form. They claim that the prefix *n* in *Nyame* (Nyawe) and *im* in *Elohim*, the latter a Hebrew word for God, both represent a plural or collective form. This Christian view, however, is not supported by the facts. The *n* in the Ashanti word *Onyame* means immensity, not plurality. And as we learned earlier from Professor Bosman, Black Africans "say it would be absurd to make any human representation of the Almighty God."[16]

More than that, the plural use of the word for God was the grammatical form used in Biblical Hebrew to address any <u>individual</u> (singular) of royal or kingly rank. Dr. David Cooper, a well-known conservative (fundamentalist) Christian theologian, admits frankly that "in the ancient Semitic world such usage ('of the plural noun for excellency, majesty') was common when subjects addressed their king or at times spoke concerning him."[17] The Hebrews, of course, could be expected to address God, who is their King of kings and Lord of lords, in no less a manner.

In summary, we can see that the Hebrew God and Creator is at the heart of Black Africans, and particularly Ashanti religious beliefs. These beliefs, moreover, relate to the total Black African culture because religion traditionally was the underlying strands which held together the fabric of its society. Brodie Cruickshank in his book, EIGHTEEN YEARS ON THE GOLD COAST OF AFRICA, affirms that "the natives of the Gold Coast generally acknowledge the existence of a Supreme Being who made and governs the world."[18] He explains that "the manner in which they regard God corresponds exactly with the account given the Assyrians who became acquainted with the god of the Hebrews [Israelites]."[19]

> **Special Note:** The Ashanti word usage in this book has been further authenticated by Mr. Billy M. Hatchson-Awuma, a native of Ghana and graduate student at University of Pennsylvania.

In ancient Israel, the belief in Almighty God was just as central as it was in Black Africa. In many ways the idea of the Priesthood came second. It was the priests who maintained the Temple, interpreted the laws, served as emissaries, and in general were responsible for giving religious direction to the early Israelite nation. Among the Ashanti and other African peoples, they traditionally played an equally important role.

To be sure, the existence of a priesthood is a rather universal phenomenon. Organized religion must have some kind of leadership if it is to function. However, one important outward symbol existed among the Ashanti priesthood which links it closely to ancient Israel. That symbol is the Breastplate worn by the high priests as a symbol of their authority including their right to represent the reigning Ashanti king or queen.

The accompanying illustration is entitled "Ashanti Ambassadors Crossing the Prah." It is a direct reproduction of an actual drawing made by Melton Prior, an illustrator for the _Illustrated London News._ He accompanied the British colonial expeditionary forces in West Africa during the famous Ashanti War of 1873-1874. The illustration first appeared in the February 14, 1874 issue of this famous British periodical, which remains in circulation to this day.[20]

A news dispatch accompanies the illustration. It explains that "our Special Artist in one of his sketches engraved for this week's paper shows the crossing of the Prah River by these (Ashanti) ambassadors on a pontoon raft accompanied by Lieutenant Grant."[21] That Melton Prior is the same "Special Artist" and that he was eye-witness to the events of this war are proven conclusively in the January 1st issue of that year. The introduction to this letter reads, "We (the Editors) have received the following letter with several sketches from Melton Prior, our Special Artist, who accompanies Sir Ganet Wolsely's expedition to Coomassie."[22]

This very same illustration by Prior also appears in COOMASSIE TO MAGDALA, a book written the same year by Sir Henry Morton Stanley.[23] For those who do not immediately recognize the name, Stanley is the famous Anglo-American explorer who joined David Livingstone to prove Lake Victoria to be the source of the Nile River. Stanley actually was not an explorer by profession but a journalist. He reported the Ashanti War for the <u>New York Herald</u> and at the same time wrote the aforementioned book about these experiences. His presence on the battlefields of the Ashanti War is verified additionally by his wife in her own book written after his death.[24]

Stanley describes the breastplate worn by the Ashanti ambassadors but simply as "A large gold-plated badge on his breast."[25] Professor A. B. Ellis, who wrote a book about his own experiences on the Gold Coast during the same period, also says the Ashanti representative "pointed to the gold plates on their breasts as being their insignia of office."[26] The exact details of this breastplate are shown in the illustration of Prior which Stanley put into his book.

Why have we so carefully documented the authenticity and reliability of the illustration by Prior? Of what importance is it as eye-witness proof of Hebrew civilization in Black West Africa? The answer is that the square breastplate worn by the Ashanti ambassaodor seated on the raft in the middle of the Prah River, in the very heart of Ashanti territory, is comprised of twelve parts or sections, just as was that breastplate worn by the Biblical priests (Exodus 28:21).

Professor Williams comments about the same illustration, which he also reproduces in his HEBREWISMS OF WEST AFRICA. He notes that "at first glance this would appear to be unquestionably a vestige of the High Priest of the Hebrews. But it is well to remember that . . . the breastplate was not peculiar to the Hebrews. It was to be found as well in Egypt and probably elsewhere. However, the divisions of the breastplate into twelve parts is certainly distinctive" as a Hebrew symbol.[27]

ASHANTI AMBASSADORS CROSSING THE PRAH

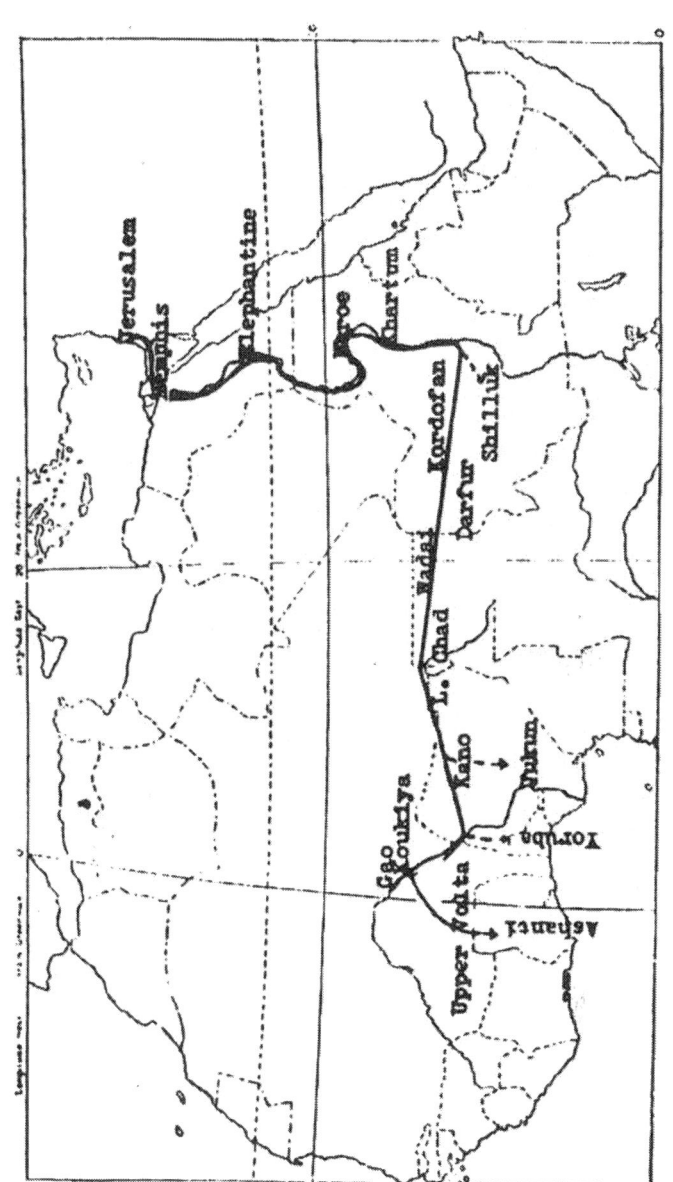

FROM NILE TO NIGER

Labels on map: Jerusalem, Elephantine, Khartum, Kordofan, Shilluk, Darfur, Wadai, L. Chad, Kano, Yoruba, Gao, Koukiya, Upper Volta, Ashanti

The accuracy and reliability of the illustration by Prior goes beyond its use by Sir Morton Stanley and Professor Williams. It also comes from the first-hand observations of T. Edward Bowditch some fifty years earlier. In his MISSION FROM CAPE COAST CASTLE TO ASHANTI, written in 1819, he notes that "one curious evidence may be added to the former identification of the Ashanti nations. It is the tradition that the whole of these people were originally comprehended into twelve tribes or families in which they classify themselves still."[28] (Of this book Sir Henry Morton Stanley says, "A more interesting book of travels I have seldom read.")[29] Dr. Friedrich Ratzel in his book, HISTORY OF MANKIND, supports this finding. He says the Ashanti nation is composed of "twelve stocks . . . the members of which are distributed randomly throughout the tribes."[30]

Besides the twelve-part breastplate worn by the Ashanti representative, the illustration reveals another symbol which also links the Ashanti directly to the Hebrews. Williams notes that " the head-dress of the herald (representative) with its gold disc in front, satisfies the description of the Hebrew miznefet."[31] The miznefet is described in the JEWISH ENCYCLOPEDIA as "a tiara or perhaps a peculiarly wound turban with a peak in the front which bore a gold plate with the inscription of 'Holy Unto Yhwh.'"[32]

Does this description of the Hebrew miznefet fit the head-dress in the Illustration by Prior? The answer upon simple observation is <u>yes</u>! The conclusion is verified by Professor Rattray who says, "The (Ashanti) head-dress of a herald is a cap made from the skin of a Colobus monkey with a gold disc in front."[33] These two prominent articles of clothing, the twelve-part breastplate and the gold disc tiara headpiece, are found as part of the priestly vestments of only one other religion; that is the Hebrew religion of Biblical days.

The striking similarities, however, do not end here. We might pause to consider some other less obvious similarities which suggest a close relationship between the religion of the Ashanti and the ancient Hebrews.

In the Bible (Exodus 3:2f), the saga of the burning bush on Mount Sinai "heralds" the beginning of the all-important Mosaic revelation climaxed by the giving of the Ten Commandments to the *Israelite* people. The Hebrew word for bush is sene.[34] Rattray tells us "the Ashanti have a myth which states that the Creator made a herald (osene), a drummer (okyerema), and an executioner (obrafo), and that the precedence of these officials in the Ashanti (royal) court is in that order."[35] Thus the Ashanti word osene, whose root is sene, is virtually identical to the Hebrew word sene. Both refer to a herald or heralding of an important revelation or event.

To support this view, we find likeness between the other two Ashanti words mentioned above and the description of the Mosaic revelation. The Ashanti word okyerema, whose root is kyerema, sounds much like the Hebrew word Khoreb, the western height of Mount Sinai. After dropping the prefix o and the suffix fo from obrafo, the second Ashanti word, we have bra which resembles the Hebrew word brith which means "covenant." The Ashanti myth might thus record the progressive stages in the manifestation of Yahweh (God) to the Hebrews: the burning bush, Mount Sinai, and the Mosaic covenant," says Williams.[36]

Besides these very basic concepts, the Mosaic Laws played an extremely important role in the development of the Judaic way of life. The best known part of these laws are the Ten Commandments, although they involve much more. The word Torah "was from an early period employed as a general term to cover all kinds of laws," according to the JUNIOR JEWISH ENCYCLOPEDIA.[37] The Law-giver in Ashanti is called Toro!

In summary, we find many striking similarities between the religion-based cultures of the Ashanti and the pre-Exilic Hebrews. These similarities are too many and too close to be accidental. We find the words and concepts for the Almighty God are identical. We find the words for Creator are identical. We find the same Sabbath (Saturday) reference. We find the same historical views of twelve tribes. We find the same twelve-part breastplate and head-dress of the priests. We find similar meanings for the words "herald" which plays an important part in both cultures. We find other concepts using similar sounding words. We find many similarities in marriage and child-birth customs both of which play very important roles in these largely agrarian societies. And we find the very same name "Ashanti" has its counterpart in ancient Israel.

It is important, however, to know that the similarities do not end with the Ashanti. They also are found among the other peoples of West Africa and of Central and East Africa, too. For more insights into the Hebraic customs of these African peoples, the next chapter digests and discusses what many scholars and eye-witnesses have to say.

Chapter Six

OTHER HEBREWISMS IN BLACK AFRICA

IN THIS CHAPTER WE DISCUSS the peoples who are the neighbors of the Ashanti in West Africa. In addition, there is a discussion of the people who inhabit other regions of Black Africa to the east and south. We have divided our survey into geographical areas roughly equivalent to the countries that make up Africa today. However, we want to make it clear once again that tribal groupings almost never fit within the boundaries of a single country. The borders were established mainly by European colonial overlords for reasons usually having to do with the ethnic affiliations of the indigenous population, some of whom are sedentary while others are nomadic.

To preface this discussion, we want to re-emphasize that "polytheistic" tendencies existed among the Israelites/Jews during different periods of their history. Dr. Nahum Slouschz says in his TRAVELS IN NORTH AFRICA that the primitive Jews of Morocco "often have a polytheistic character" about their worship "which often approaches fetichism. There still (in 1927) are some who worship grottoes, and rocks and stones under the guise of saints." [1] The reason we mention this polytheistic tendency among the Berber Jews of North Africa is to remind our reader that such reversions or abberations have not disqualified these people from being "reclaimed" as members of the reborn State of Israel where they are full-fledged citizens.

With this brief introduction, we can better resume our investigation of the cultural and religious affinities between Black African and Middle East Hebrew civilizations.

Guinea

The observations of J. Leighton Wilson are especially worthy of our attention for any study of this region. The reason is because he was a missionary in the Guinean area for about 18 years. His book, WESTERN AFRICA: ITS HISTORY, CONDITION AND PROSPECTS, was published in 1856 before Christianity had an opportunity to make an impact upon the culture and religion of the region. In the preface of his book, he says that "the great body of the book is the result of my own observations and knowledge."[2]

He records in his book that "there are many obvious traces of Judaism, both in Northern and Southern Guinea." He says further that "in Northern Guinea paganism and Judaism are united."[3] He then explains that in the Northern region the practice of Judaism is prominently developed, some of the leading features of which are circumcision, the division of tribes into separate families, and very frequently into the number twelve; blood sacrifices with the sprinkling of blood upon the altars and doorposts" and other customs he classified of Israelite origin.[4]

Dr. William Bosman in his book about his travels in Guinea observes that the women of this region must accept an oath-drink to acquit themselves of any accusation of adultery. The law is that sickness or death which follows the taking of this drink is evidence of guilt. Bosman claims that "this drink seems very much like the bitter water administered to the women of the Old Testament by way of acquitting them of the charge of adultery."[5]

Elsewhere in his book Bosman says "The Negroes still

retain several laws and customs which savour of Judaism, as their marrying of their brother's wife after his death, and several more. They seem the same in effect, as well as the names, of which here (in Guinea) are several which occur in the Old Testament."[6]

Mungo Park, in his book entitled TRAVELS IN THE INTERIOR DISTRICTS OF AFRICA, written in 1810, observes the legal whippings among the Teesee people in the Kassob region. He says "the number of stripes was precisely the same as are required by Mosaic Law -- forty, save one." He also notes that these people were neither Christian nor Moslem at that time.[7]

In the same book, Park relates that "on the first appearance of the New Moon the natives say a short prayer . . . to the Supreme Being. This prayer is pronounced in a whisper, the party holding up his hands before his face. This ceremony seems to be nearly the same which prevailed among the Hebrews in the days of Job."[8]

It is significant to heed the words of Rabbi Kaufman Kohler in his JEWISH ENCYCLOPEDIA article on the New Moon. He maintains "the period of the New Moon in pre-exilic times . . . was superior even to the Sabbath day, which formed but a part of it, but lost its importance during the Exile (which began about 586 B.C.E. (B.C.))." He also says in the same article that "in the temple, the New Moon was celebrated by special sacrifices and by the blowing of the shofar (ram's horn)."[9]

Dahomey

Professor Melville Herskovitz, one of the most distinguished American anthropologists[10] from Northwestern University, writes about the Ewe of Dahomey and Togo. This tribe, pronounced _ava_, with long vowel "a's", represents one of the two major peoples in this region. He notes that "in the life of the Dahomian Mawu is but another Vodu or Yehwe, the two terms being synonymous."[11] He says elsewhere that

"Mawu is but another Vodu or Yehwe, a generic term for Great God."[12]

Although his phonetic spelling differs somewhat, J. S. Sketcherly writing about DAHOMEY AS IS confirms that "their Supreme Being is called Mahu or Mahu-no, and is vested with unlimited authority over every being, both spiritual and carnal."[13]

Bishop Auguste Herman, in a series of articles about the Ewe people among whom he lived, provides us with a most revealing insight into their beliefs as they compare with those of the ancient Hebrews:

He says, "This cult of Mahou presents certain particulars which resemble survivals of primitive religion of a Hebrew tradition. It teaches its followers a high idea of purity and sanctity of God. Its ministers are clothed in white cloth. They observe the laws of continence prescribed to Israelite priests when they served in the Temple. Strict rules mark the periods when women participate in the rites of the cult. The water intended for ritual blessings can be brought only by a young woman who is a virgin. The official day of rest is Saturday. On that day the followers of Mahou (Almighty God) do not work in the fields. Once a year they offer a solemn sacrifice in an enclosure, outside the village. The priest takes in his hands a sheep which must be white. Three times he raises it toward the heavens. A part of the soup (made from the slain lamb) is poured on the ground as an offering to God."[14]

Herman rhetorically asks: "This purification, this triple oblation of the sacrifice, this sacred repast in common, this Saturday sanctified by rest, does not all this recall old Biblical tradition?"[15] Obviously his answer is yes!

Professor Williams, in his ANTHROPOLOGICAL SERIES published by Boston College Graduate School in 1936 and 1937, talks about a map published in the 1970 edition of the MEM-

OIRS OF THE REIGN OF BASSA AHADEE, KING OF DAHOMEY, by Robert Norris. It is an eye-witness account. The map which it contains designates the region surrounding the seaport town of Whyday as the "Country of the Jews.' In fact, the name of the town very much sounds like Judah.[16] The spelling usually found today is Ouidah, with the "o" sound dropped. Here we have an actual illustrated designation of a Hebrew population living in the very heart of the Black African slave coast.

The importance of this Dahomian coastal town is explained by Sir Richard Burton, another famous explorer of the last century. He says "about the middle of the 17th century it rose to the rank of a prosperous ivory mart and slave port." [17] This is reported thirty years earlier by John Atkins, who says, "Whydah is the greatest trading place on the Coast of Guinea (as the area was called in those days by the Europeans)." [18]

The existence of an active Jewish community in Dahomey is reported much later by an educated native of the Whydah region whose name is Bata Kindai Amgoza. He wrote a series of articles for the now defunct SCRIBNER'S MAGAZINE in 1929 which appeared the following year in the form of a book. He informs his readers that the "B'nai Ephraim . . . have part of the Hebrew Torah . . . in a sacred place." He also says "they have clung to the old Jewish traditions, to the laws of Moses, to the great Biblical holy days, to circumcision, to the worship of Yehovah, and to the hierarchial rule of rabbis." They are described in the introduction to the book as "dark in color, unclothed, like the (other) natives) who surround them." [19]

Dr. J. Kreppel, in his book about Jews and Judaism, also reports a large Jewish community in the interior of Dahomey. He says, "They have a central temple and a Pentateuch [Torah] written in Hebrew letters." [20]

We find reference to still another map, the existence of which confirms the basic integrity of the one by Norris mentioned above. Pierre Bouche, a French historian, makes reference in his 1885 book to an earlier map by Jean D'Anville which indicates that the country around Nagos formerly was inhabited by Jews.[21] He says this view was found still earlier in the writings of Idrisi, an Arab scholar and geographer of the 12th Century. He adds: "One finds among the Blacks many Jewish customs."[22]

Ghana

We already have discussed at some length the Ashanti who live in and about Ghana. We want to add what Reverend Christian Reindorf of the Basel Mission has to say about the high priest of the Akra people who inhabit the Gold Coast, as it was then called. He asserts, "A close inspection of the priest in his officiating garb leads to the conviction that his worship must be of foreign origin. . . . One is inclined to suppose that the Jewish [Israelite] system of worship in the Old Testament style has been either introduced by or imitated from the people who came out first to the (Gold) Coast." [23] He obviously has reference to priestly vestments very similar to, if not the same as, those worn by the Ashanti priests.

Nigeria

G. T. Basden was for many years a missionary among the Ibo. These people live mainly in the southeastern region of modern Nigeria, though they can be found scattered throughout the entire country. Because these people are largely non-Muslems, it is likely their ancestors were among the slaves transported to America and the West Indies.

According to Basden, in his book entitled AMONG THE IBO OF NIGERIA, "There are certain customs which point to

Levitic [Israelite] influence at a more or less remote time. This is suggested by the underlying ideas concerning sacrifice and in the practice of circumcision. The language also bears several interesting parallels with Hebrew idiom."[24] He later notes that "Among the Ibo people there is a distinct recognition of a Supreme Being beneficent in character who is above every other spirit, good or evil. He is believed to control all things in heaven and on earth, and dispenses rewards and punishments according to merit."[25]

In fact, the Hebrew concept of One God also is part of the indigenous culture of the Yoruba, another very important ethnic group in Nigeria. The Yoruba, like the Ibo, live mainly in the coastal states of modern-day Nigeria adjacent to the Ewe and Akan (Ashanti) peoples of neighboring Dahomey and Ghana. Robert Collins, in his AFRICAN ENCOUNTER: A DOCTOR IN NIGERIA, gives us a clue not merely of the basic concept of native Yoruba belief, but also its subsequent development. He explains, "The Yoruba believed in an Infinite God which could not be described in finite terms or approached directly, so they invented a mythology of deities, each of them representing different aspects of human experience."[26]

Here, in Yoruba theology, we find another similarity to traditional Israelite practice which dates back to the days of the old priesthood. Rabbi Gerson D. Cohen, in his contribution to GREAT AGES AND IDEAS OF THE JEWISH PEOPLE, states that "His (God's) very name (was) taboo to all but the high priest, who uttered it only on the Day of Atonement. So awesome was His name, so wary was the Jew of taking it in vain, that even <u>Elohim</u> (God) was not employed in conversation, nor even the euphemistic <u>Adonai</u> (Lord)."[27] To this very day, Orthodox Jews spell God as "G-d" in deference to this tradition.

BETA ISRAEL (FALASHA): THE BLACK JEWS OF ETHIOPIA

The NATIONAL JEWISH MONTHLY

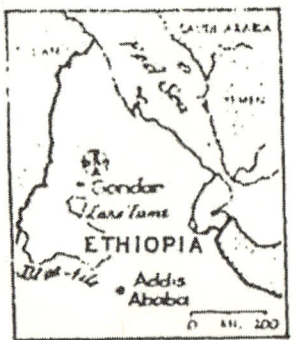

The New York Times   Feb. 4, 1973
The area of the Falashas
is near Gondar (cross).

BETA ISRAEL (FALASHA):
THE BLACK JEWS OF ETHIOPIA

The NATIONAL JEWISH MONTHLY

TEMPLE BETH EL - VIRGINIA

West Africa

AFRICAN JEWS

Ethiopia

48

AFRO-AMERICAN HEBREW LEADERS

HEBREW EDUCATION

Besides the Ibo and Yoruba, we also find reference to Judaism in the northern half of the country populated today largely by Hausa and Fulani, the latter sometimes spelled Feul or Peul. Edmond D. Morel devotes considerable space to the Fulani in his book, AFFAIRS OF WEST AFRICA. He concludes that after the overthrow of the Hyksos rulers of Egypt, many of their Hebrew kinsmen found their way into the interior of Africa by way of Cyrenaica (Libya).[28] He remarks a few pages later that "The Hebraic flavor, if one may put it so, which seem to permeate many of the Fulani customs . . . has been recorded by many observers."[29]

Maurice Abadie, a French historian, asserts that "The Semitic origin of the Fulani of the Niger . . . cannot be questioned." [30] He believes Jews from North Africa also joined their brethren many years later in the Second Century C.E. (A.D.) to found the Empire of Ghana.[31] Professor Williams thinks it therefore is not surprising to find the Fulani also living in the neighboring lands of the Cameroons and Senegal.[32]

Senegal and Gambia

Perhaps more revealing are the comments which Edmond Morel makes in his book about the experiences of his friend, Captain de Guiraudon, who lived for several years among the Fulani in the Senegal-Gambia region or Senegambia, as it once was called. Morel says that Guiraudon "was particularly struck by their peculiar knowledge of Jewish history. So familiarly did they speak of the chief Hebrew personalities of the Old Testament, and so well posted were they with the principle events related in it that they could not . . . have acquired their knowledge through Arabic sources which place little emphasis on such matters.

"They referred," Morel continues, "to those times as

though dealing with their own national records. Moses and Abraham might have been individuals of the same race as themselves. (Morel then quotes Guiraudon that 'in their oral legends Moses plays a very important part, and although certain passages of the Scripture are transformed, or rather assimilated, they have so intense a Biblical and Hebraic tone as to exclude all Arabic influence.')" The strongest evidence of their direct relationship to a Hebrew past rests in the fact, as Guiraudon himself notes, "that their Israelite chronicles ceased after Solomon."[33]

Guiraudon's conclusions are best summarized in his own words. He says, "It would seem as if the Fulani . . . were at least in permanent contact with the Israelite people in remote times." [34] Morel concludes that the Fulani "are the lineal descendants of the Hyksos" whom he identifies as Hebrews, "having migrated westward with the overthrow of the Shepherd conquerors (of Egypt). . . . Their presence in West Africa dates back at least 2,500 years."[35]

Central Africa (Congo, Angola, Kenya, etc.)

In Chapter Three we noted that scholars believe there is a common origin for the Ashanti and Bantu peoples. They both came, it is thought, from the northeastern part of the African continent. The Ashanti eventually migrated to the west coast roughly parallel to the southern edge of the Sahara Desert. The Bantu, by contrast, moved mainly to the south so that today they occupy nearly the entire southern half of the continent from the Congo Republic and Zaire on the west to Mozambique on the east and southward to the very southernmost tip called the Cape of Good Hope.

Because most Black Americans are not related directly to the Bantu, we will abbreviate our discussion about them. However, their significance should not be overlooked, either, historically. Our knowledge of their Hebrew traditions simply confirms and reinforces what we already know about West Africa: that the Hebrew strain exists in Black Africa far more extensively than most people realize.

In the Congo River region there exists a remarkable affinity of certain customs with ancient Hebrew law, says Herbert Ward in his book, A VOICE FROM THE CONGO. He notes, for example, that "if adultery is committed within the village, both the man and the woman are considered equally guilty; outside the village boundary, however, the man only is held at fault." [36] Professor A. G. Keller of Yale University reports that many West African funeral customs are in the same class with the ritual "sackcloth and ashes" of the Old Testament.[37]

Farther south, in Angola, we learn from Professor Merlin Ennis in his writings about the Ovimbundu that "there are many indications that there was as least a common source from which arose the Hebrew culture; and that this (Angolan culture) arose from that. There are many place names in Palestine and more especially in the eastern end of the Arabian peninsula (which also was inhabited by Jews in pre-Islamic times) that resemble Bantu names." [38] It should be noted that the Ovimbundu represent one of the major ethnic groups in Angola. Dr. Friedrich Ratzel speaks of the Mavumba as "renowned potters and smiths to whom some assign a Jewish origin." [39]

John Clarke, a British missionary, writes in 1848 that Oldendorf, an earlier traveler in the region previously called French Equatorial Africa, and now known in part as the Central African republic, "speaks of Black Jews being in this part of Africa," too.[40]

Father Guiseppe Clattl spent several years at the Kaheti Catholic Mission in Kenya. In a manuscript written in September, 1932, he says, "It can be easily concluded that the Agekoyo have had some contact with the Hebrews after their departure from Egypt."[41]

He then explains: Leviticus 28:1-23 "is rigorous law for the Agekoyo." Exodus 21:35,36 "is scrupulously observed." The same he says of Exodus 22:10, 13, 18, 22, and Exodus 23:4, 19, 22 which "are fully observed precisely as written." Leviticus 19:14, 26, 32, 33 "are also laws of the tribe."[42]

In summary, we see that Hebrew religion and culture permeated Black Africa from coast to coast, and represents the very heart of the native civilization, however much it may have changed or become corrupted through the centuries. The interactions occurred when close personal contacts were inevitable. No radio, no television, no other means of instant or remote communications had been invented. As a consequence, there can be no doubt about the close personal contact made between the peoples of Black Africa and those from the ancient Hebrew Middle East. This in itself gives logic to the view that Black Africa is made of Hebrew blood besides being rooted in its culture.

We have concentrated our analysis thus far on comparisons between Black African culture and the Biblical Hebrew civilization of so-called pre-Exilic times. The centuries before the first exile of the Israelites from the Holy Land occurred about 586 B.C.E. (B.C.). This was when the first Temple in Jerusalem was destroyed and the Israelite inhabitants -- at least a large portion of them -- were led into exile and forced to settle in Babylonia. The periods before the exile include the reigns of Kings Saul, David and Solomon, and the exodus under the leadership of Moses about 1225 B.C.E. (B.C.)

The major reason we have directed our attention to a period in history when the Temple priesthood still flourished, is to establish that the ancestors of most Black Americans are related to and part of the "parent stock" commonly called the "Original Israelites." We do not wish to minimize the importance of other aspects and periods of Black African history, such as the events which led to the establishment of the famous Ghanian and Songui empires in later centuries. However, any attempt to tell this part of African history would require many more pages.

The remainder of our book, therefore, is devoted to a discussion of the "human links" between Black Africa and the Hebrew Middle East, particularly during Biblical times. It is a discussion which dates back to the Patriarch of all the Hebrews -- the first Hebrew -- whose name was Abraham, the father of the Israelites. In this way, we hope to contribute to a better understanding of history, particularly by Black people, whose spiritual and cultural re-awakening has just begun to bud again.

Chapter Seven

AFRICAN HEBREWS:
THE OFFSPRING OF ABRAHAM

THIS CHAPTER IS DEVOTED MAINLY to establishing the human links between the Middle East and Africa, especially that region of the later known as Black West Africa. We determined in previous chapters that Hebrew beliefs and customs are foundation-stones of Black African civilizations. We also saw how the migrations tended to move from east to west. Obviously none of this happened by magic or by accident. It happened as a consequence of historic events. Warfare forced people to move; droughts and floods had their effect upon people dependent on the soil for their survival. And the continuing search for more space and better land spurred migrations, too.

For these reasons, we will explore some of the evidence we have about these migrations of people in Africa, particularly those which started in the Middle East and found their ways to the Atlantic shores of West Africa. We have used the word "migrations" in the plural to lend credence to the fact that Hebrew penetration into the heart and soul of Africa came in waves over a long period of time. At best, we must arbitrarily divide these overlapping movements for the sake of historical convenience.

It is impossible and certainly impractical in any event to deal with each and every surge of migration from the Middle East into Africa. We lack the necessary records, in the first instance. But we do want to highlight some of the more important early ones, especially those which are tied to well-known personalities of that time.

We turn to Professor Samuel A. B. Mercer, an expert in Biblical history, to start our investigation. He informs us, in his EXTRA-BIBLICAL SOURCES FOR HEBREW AND JEWISH HISTORY, that "about 1650 B.C.E. (B.C.) Jacob and his family went into Egypt and stayed there, according to Biblical tradition, for about 430 years." [1] What the author is saying is that Hebrews settled in Egypt no later than 1650 B.C.E., or 3,650 years ago, and remained there at least until 1220 B.C.E. (B.C.), when Moses led them out of bondage.

According to Professor Mercer, "This was a time of great migrations; and we find the Hyksos, a Semitic people, a branch of whom Jacob and his family may well have been, entered Egypt and became rulers of the land." In support of his conclusion that Semites once ruled Egypt, Mercer observes that "scarabs of a Hyksos ruler gave his name as Jacob-her or Jacob-el," the latter name a common Hebrew appelation meaning "God of Jacob." [2]

Dr. Henry Orlinsky, a professor of Bible at the Hebrew Union College-Jewish Institute of Religion, says the word "Hyksos" means "rulers of foreign countries." [3] To the ancient Egyptians, that meant people who came from the Middle East from across the Nile River. This view is shared by most historians. Professor Williams believes that "the Pharoah who showed friendship to Joseph and his (Hebrew) brethren must really have belonged to the (same) shepherd race. This fact might easily explain the enmity and persecution to which the Hebrews were subjected after the expulsion of their kinsfolk, the Hyksos (about 1580 B.C.E.)" [4]

In summary, then, we find that the Hebrews reached Africa no later than 1650 B.C.E. (B.C.) or more than 3,600 years ago. Their presence in Egypt, which began peacefully under so-called Hyksos rule, eventually deteriorated through discrimination, persecution and ultimate bondage. They once again regained their freedom about 1220 B.C.E. (B.C.) under the leadership of Moses.

It is clear, however, that not everyone left Egypt with Moses, contrary to popular opinion. Professor Sidney Mendelssohn, in his book entitled JEWS IN AFRICA, tells us that "When the children of Israel crossed the Red Sea . . . the exodus was by no means universal."[5] Edmond Fleg, in his book about the life of Moses, observes that there is, in fact, a rabbinic tradition that "many Israelites . . . remained with the Egyptians"[6] at the time of the famous Mosaic exodus.

What happened to those Israelites who remained in Egypt, or more generally, in Africa, after the exodus northward into the *Wilderness of Sinai,* led by Moses? The answer seems to be two-fold. First, many remained in Egypt, as Mendelssohn and Fleg tell us. Others migrated south and westward into the heart of Africa, as Williams and other scholars say.

Edward D. Morel, in his AFFAIRS OF WEST AFRICA, informs us that the Fulani and related West Africans are the "lineal descendants" of the Hyksos and other related Hebrew migrants.[7] Williams says, "The gradual migration of the *Israelites* is perhaps the simplest, if not the only, plausible explanation" for finding a Black Hebrew culture in West Africa and in the Bantu country in the southern half of the continent.[8] These conclusions, in turn, are affirmed by the fact that scholars report that the ancestors of the Fulani, Ashanti, Ewe, Yoruba, Bantu and other ethnic groups traveled the very same migration routes.[9]

Another important period of Israelite migration into Africa was climaxed during the reign of King Solomon whose rule ended about 975 B.C.E., or some 500 years after the Mosaic exodus. It was during the reign of Solomon that Israelite influence was greatly extended as a result of his numerous marital and political alliances in Ethiopia, the Sudan and neighboring lands.

Although some historians differ in certain particulars, the Ethiopians believe themselves descended from the earlier inhabitants of the ancient kingdom established by Solomon and the Queen of Sheba, in part through their son, Bayna-Lehkem or Menelik, as he also is called.

Confirmation of this native Ethiopian theory about their own origins comes from F. Balthazar Tellez who wrote in 1710 that "There were always Jews in Ethiopia from the beginning."[10]   Professor Sidney Mendelssohn says in his book, "This statement (by Tellez) may be conjecturally justified by the proximity of Abyssinia, Ethiopia and their dependencies to the ancient homes of the Israelites in Egypt and Palestine."[11]

In fact, Sir Walter Plowden, British Consul General to Ethiopia in 1868, maintains, "Two things are certain: that at a far later period (after Solomon) six sovereigns of pure *Hebrew stock* and Jewish faith reigned at Gondor (Ethiopia). . . . I think it also highly probable that the whole of Abyssinia was of the Jewish persuasion previous to its conversion to Christianity in the Fourth Century C.E. (A.D.)."[12]

Louis J. Morie, a noted French historian, thinks the Falasha Jews of Ethiopia derive from the Israelite tribe of Levi.[13] The word "Falasha" is the name commonly given Ethiopians who practice Judaism.   The historian, Job Leutholf, who wrote in the 17th century, says the word Falasha means *"Exiles,"* to designate that they came from the Holy Land.[14] And many scholars, says Dr. George A. Barton in his JEWISH ENCYCLOPEDIA contribution, believe "they derive from exiles, possibly after the destruction of the Northern Kingdom (of Israel), but more probably from Judea after the destruction of Jerusalem by the Romans."[15]

The Bible provides us with still more evidence that Israelites lived in Ethiopia and the Sudan as far back as 725 B.C.E. (B.C.). The prophet Isaiah, who lived at that time, prophesied that ". . . The LORD shall set forth His hand a second time to recover the remnant of His people . . . from Assyria, and from Egypt, and from Pathros [southernmost Egypt, known as Nubia], and from Cush [now Ethiopia and the Sudan]."[16] (See Isaiah 11:11.) Only 70 years later another Hebrew prophet, Zephaniah (in 3:10) was to say, "From beyond the rivers of Ethiopia my suppliants, even the daughter of My dispersed, shall bring Mine offering."[17]

That an Israelite population already inhabited the inland heart of black Africa is recorded by John Africanus, a famous 16th century geographer and historian. He records in his book, which in translation is entitled A GEOGRAPHICAL HISTORY OF AFRICA, "There inhabiteth a most populous nation of Jewish stock" located west of the Nile and below the Sahara in a region between "Abassin [Ethiopia] and Congo."[18] A glance at any modern map shows that the region which Africanus says was inhabited by Jews at the time of Menelik, son of Solomon and the Queen of Sheba [Makéda], is almost precisely the "Chad-Nile" area from where Dixon[19] and other scholars[20] inform us the "parent stock" of today's Black Africans came, bringing with them the Hebrew customs of their forefathers, as we already have seen.

At this point in our discussion it might be worth noting that most historians agree that the early Israelites bear little, if any, resemblance to the white European Jews of today. This very fact should help us grasp the idea that non-whites, at least by today's standards, could not be related by blood and culture to the earliest Israelites.

The conclusion that most white Jews do not stem from Israelites in the racial sense is affirmed, for example, by Professor Karl Kautsky in his book, ARE THE JEWS A RACE? He summarizes the situation as follows: "A mixed race from the start, the Jews in the course of their migrations have come into contact with a great succession of new races, and their blood has become more and more mixed."[21]

Kautsky informs us that "as early as 139 B.C.E. (B.C.) Jews were deported from Rome because they made proselytes in Italy. It is reported in Antioch (in modern-day Turkey) that the majority of the Jewish congregation in town consisted of converts to Judaism, not of Jews by birth. Conditions," he says, "must have been so similar in many other places. This fact alone shows the absurdity of the effort to explain traits of the (white) Jews on the basis of their race."[22]

An Oxford University scholar, Professor Griffith Taylor, writes, "There is, of course, little relationship between the original Semitic Jews of the Middle East and the Slavic Jews of Poland and vicinity." This diversity, he explains, results "mainly by an extensive proselytizing movement among the southern Russians in the early centuries of our era." Taylor concludes that the "Jews are not a race, but only a people."[23]

Professor Eugene Pittard, in his well-known book, RACE AND HISTORY, summarizes the ethnic situation of white Jews in this way: "It seems . . . that the least informed reader will come to the conclusion that no Jewish race exists in the zoological sense of the word. The Jews constitute a religious and social community, certainly very strong and coherent; but its (racial) elements are heterogeneous in the extreme."[24]

Even the Biblical evidence which we have points to a mixing of peoples at an early time. Judah, the son of Jacob, took a Canaanite wife (Genesis 38:2). Joseph Married an Egyptian woman (Genesis 4:45). Sampson had wives from several different nations, including the daughter of an Egyptian Pharoah (I Kings 3:1). And his son, Roboam, who was to succeed him, was born of an Ammonite mother (I Kings 14:31). With all these women, it is highly doubtful if any ever formally converted to Judaism, in the modern sense of the word.

In retrospect, we see that the Hebrews were a diverse people almost from the start. They had no single ethnic background. Because we know that the Black African heritage is rooted deeply in this ancient and diverse stock, it therefore should not be surprising to discover that the very first Hebrews -- those who started with and accompanied Abraham -- were themselves black, at least in the contemporary definition of the terms. That Abraham and his followers were black not only is plausible in modern-day terms of color and race, *but* it is also supported by certain Biblical discoveries relating to that period some 4,000 years ago.

We know that the Bible serves as a source of religious inspiration. It also is a treasure chest of historical information which at times must be deciphered. In this connection, we might examine the Biblical account given in Genesis 10:8-10 which says that "Cush begat Nimrod (whose) kingdom was Babel, Erech, Accad, and Calneh, in the land of Shinar." This means, according to the ENCYCLOPEDIA AMERICANA section on "Nimrod," that he "was a Cushite, that he established the kingdom of Shinar (about 2450 B.C.E.), the classic Babylonia, (and) extended his kingdom along the Tigris River over Assyria."[25]

The meaning of the word "Cush" used in the definition in the above paragraph is explained by W. Max Muller, professor of Bible Exegesis, in his discussion of "Cushite" in the JEWISH ENCYCLOPEDIA. He says the word means "the ancestors of the Nubians," who today inhabit southernmost Egypt and parts of the Sudan and Ethiopia, three nations on the African continent.[26] More generally, the word is used to designate people of Black African origin. Thus we have proof that Nimrod, king of the Asian kingdom of Shinar, or Babylonia, was himself of Black African descent.

The Bible tells us something else of great importance to our discussion. It informs us that the Asiatic land of Assyria, which included ancient Babylonia, also was known as Ethiopia, just like its modern African nation counterpart. This fact is confirmed in Genesis 2:13, which says that the Gihon River "borders Ethiopia." Where is the Gihon River? It flows through "Central Asia (and) forms the Russian-Afganistan border, flowing through *the former* Turkmen Soviet Socialist Republic and through Uzbek Soviet Socialist Republic to (the) Aral Sea," says the COLUMBIA LIPPINCOTT GAZETEER OF THE WORLD, published by the Columbia University Press.[27]

According to the NEW COLUMBIA ENCYCLOPEDIA, this river, now called by its Russian name, the Amu Darya, "figured importantly in the history of Persia and in the campaigns of Alexander the Great."[28] It concerns us mainly because it was one of the northern borders of ancient Assyria, which we learned is called Ethiopia in the Bible and includes Shinar, otherwise known as ancient Babylonia.

Thus, a distinction must be made between the two Ethiopias. In Bible times, the word had reference to both Babylonia in Asia and Cush, or Nubia, in Africa. Today the word is used only to describe the modern African nation of the same name.

The Bible, in Genesis 2:11-12, also calls Babylonia by still another name (besides Shinar); it is called the "Land of Havilah." According to the section on this subject in the ENCYCLOPEDIA AMERICANA, referennce to Havilah is to a region that "was inhabited by the sons of Cush."[29] In other words, Babylonia during the time of King Nimrod was known variously as Shinar, Ethiopia, and Havilah, the last two words in particular signifying rule and inhabitation by Cushites, people of Black African origin.

Most scholars place the Kingdom of Shinar along the

Persian Gulf shores which extend from the Tigris-Euphrates River Delta in Iran and Iraq into the northern reaches of the Arabian Peninsula.

A. H. Sayce, Professor of Assyriology at Oxford University, notes that the Bible in Micah 5:6 uses the terms "land of Assyria" and "land of Nimrod" as synonymous or duplicates of each other, as is common in Biblical grammar. Once again, we have reference to Nimrod having a domain known as Assyria, bordered on the north by the Gihon River and including the Kingdom of Babylonia, which extended into the Arabian Peninsula.[30]

The fact that Black people lived in southern Babylonia along the shores of the Persian Gulf is verified by archeology. Dr. George G. Cameron of the Department of Oriental Studies at the University of Chicago tells us in his HISTORY OF EARLY IRAN that there is "evidence that a protonegroid population once extended westward from India [now Pakistan] along the shores of the Persian Gulf."[31] The word "*protonegroid*" means *early or ancient Black people*, the prefix "*proto*" being defined in the AMERICAN COLLEGE DICTIONARY as "a word element meaning '*first*,' or '*earliest form of.*'"

Sir Harry Johnston, the noted authority on Black anthropology and culture, observes, "There is a curliness of the hair, together with a negro eye and full lips in the portraiture of Assyria which conveys the idea of an evident negro element in Babylonia." His meaning could not be clearer! He also makes reference in the same section of his book to "the Asiatic negroid strain of Jews," undoubtedly his reference to those living in the Persian Gulf area.[32]

Thus we have independent scholarly documentation that a negroid or black population lived in ancient Babylonia, ruled by King Nimrod about 2450 B.C.E. (B.C.). The question arises, Why does the Bible put such emphasis on the Ethiopic origin of King Nimrod and his kingdom by giving names to

Babylonia which have Black African connotations? And what has this to do with the "original *Hebrews or* Israelites"? The answer is that the reign or dynasty of King Nimrod coincides with certain written records about Abraham, traditionally the first Hebrew, and Ur, the city-state in which Abraham was recorded to have been born and lived.

According to both Arabic and Jewish histories, King Nimrod plays an important role in the early life of Abraham. In the Babylonian Talmudic writings of the Jews, we find reference to King Nimrod wanting possession of the child Abraham from the latter's father, Terah.[33] This is mentioned and confirmed by Max Seligsohn, editor of the JEWISH ENCYCLOPEDIA, who writes that "Nimrod at the head of a small(?) army of Cushites attacked and defeated the Japheth-ites, after which he made Terah his minister."[34]

In Arabic history Terah also is portrayed as the chief minister of state or grand vizier of King Nimrod. A. H. Sayce says, "A statement of the Arabic writer-historian, Yo-kut, is that Hawil was the dialect spoken" by the descendants of Midian, a son of Abraham.[35] The word *Havilah,* from which *Hawil* derives, refers to land inhabited by Cushites, or Black people.

More generally, Alfred Louis Kroeber, professor of Anthropology at the University of California, notes that "some scholars find similarities between the Sumerian of Early Babylonia and Modern African languages."[36] This observation, while not universally held, lends some additional credence to the more specific findings that the dialect of Abraham's family was of African origin.

Still another fact ties Nimrod to Abraham. It is that the city-state of Ur, *birthplace* of Abraham, was located in the southern plain of Babylonia very near the shores of the Persian Gulf and the boundary of modern Arabia. George Cameron says, with reference to the years 2500 to 2200 B.C.E.

(B.C.) that "The influence of Ur reigned supreme" in Babylonia.[37] This period coincides almost precisely with the time when King Nimrod established his dynasty in this very same area.

Although it is difficult to postulate the exact circumstances about the lives of individuals in antiquity, it seems plausible that one of the motives for Abraham to leave his home in Ur was the royal court intrigues to which he was subjected. These, of course, could have resulted from the revolutionary religious ideas which he held and propogated. That Abraham himself came from rich and influential circumstances can be gleaned from Genesis 13:2, which says, "Abraham was very rich in cattle, in gold, and in silver" when he went to Egypt to get permission from the Pharoah to settle in the land of Canaan.

In summary, we find considerable evidence that Abraham came from the ruling classes of a Cushite or Black dynasty founded by King Nimrod, and that the region under their rule, particularly that part near the Persian Gulf, was inhabited by Black people. We have historical evidence, both Biblical and other, to support the conclusion that his father was an important minister in the court of this monarch and that the language used was a Cushite (African) tongue.

The Bible tends to confirm this view elsewhere in its pages. The *vision* of Daniel (7:9), written in Babylonia, refers to the "Ancient of Days" whose garment was snow-white and "the hair on his head was like pure wool." Some scholars give this an allegorical meaning. However, it most certainly describes a proto-Hebrew in its reference to the "Ancient of Days" in the anthropomorphic sense. In all likelihood it refers to Abraham himself, because he is considered the prototype of all Israelites. In any event, one thing is certain: it is a physical description which fits a Black person. Who else has wooly hair!

Even though we can link Abraham to the Cushite dynasty of King Nimrod, the question remains about his relationship to the Semites. If Abraham was Black, of African descent, could he also be a Semite? The answer is *yes,* because the word *Semite* has come to mean something different today from what it originally did. Historically, the ancient Semites were not a single or unified race, but a group of disparate ethnic groups with a common cultural background.

Dr. Allen H. Godbey, Professor of Bible at Duke University, says, "There is no such thing as a Semitic race. We use the term *Semitic* to describe a type of language and a sort of culture which we can trace by means of that type of language."[38] We find an example of this in Genesis 10:22 of the Bible where it says that the Elamites were "children" of the Semites. Most scholars reject the literal meaning and accept the view expressed in THE BIBLICAL WORLD that the relationship meant by the word "children" represents a "cultural fusion" between the two groups.[39]

Because it is culture and not race which determines who is a Semite, it is obvious that there can be dark-skinned Semites of Cushite or negroid origin.

The question naturally arises, Is there indigenous Black African tradition that parallels the conclusion that Abraham and the "original Israelites" are "parent stock" of the inhabitants of Black West Africa? The answer is "Yes!" There is native Black African tradition found among the Yoruba which is nearly identical. This important ethnic group which lives mainly in modern-day Nigeria represents, together with the Ashanti and Ewe, the largest portion of Black slaves brought to the New World.

The Yoruba tradition to which we refer is found in a book by Sultan Muhammad Bello entitled INFAQ AL-MAYRUR, later paraphrased and translated into English by E.

J. Arnett, in THE RISE OF THE SOKOTO FULANI. Bello, who lived from 1779 to 1837, was the first Fulani ruler of Sokoto, a neighboring Hausa of northern Nigeria, and a scholar in his own right.

Sultan Bello records that "The people of Yoruba descended from the Bani Kan'an and the Kindred of Nimrod. Now the reason for their having settled in the West of Africa, according to what we are told (by them), is that Ya'rub ibn Qahtan drove them from Iraq [then called Babylonia] westwards, and they traveled between Mistr and Habash until they reached Yoruba. It happened that they left a portion of their people in every country they passed."[40]

Let us examine the words of Bello closely; they represent native Yoruba historic tradition. He says this is "what we are told" by them. The Yoruba describe themselves as <u>Bani Kan'an</u>, the People from Canaan, the ancient Hebrew homeland. Just as the Bible links the earliest *Hebrew* origins to Nimrod and Babylonia, so, too, does Yoruba tradition. This same Yoruba tradition tells of migrating through Habash. This place name is also spelled "el Habesh," and is located in Ethiopia. It talks about "a portion" of their people remaining in the lands through which they traveled, which could refer not only to people in Ethiopia and the Sudan, but to the neighboring Ashanti and other nearby peoples, as well.

The tradition of a Middle East origin also is supported by the fact that the Yoruba, like their Ashanti neighbors, employ the word <u>ob</u>, which means *soothsayer* or *wizard*. We learned in Chapter Three of this book that the word is found in the Bible to describe a soothsayer from who King Saul sought advice (as was common in his day). The Yoruba use of the word <u>Oba</u> is the title of their kings or chiefs. Basil Davidson, the historian and consultant to the national Geographic Society on Africa, explains in his HISTORY OF WEST AFRICA TO THE NINETEENTH CENTURY that the king or chief used magic to prove his spiritual powers and thus to enhance or consolidate his political position. Thus he became the master magician as well as political leader.[41]

Moreover, the Yoruba, like the Ashanti, retain the concept of One God, omniscient, invisible, who cannot be depicted in human or animal form. This concept distinguished the ancient Hebrews from all their neighbors in the Middle East. It also distinguished them from their neighbors in Arabia and the Nile River Valley as they migrated through Africa.

There is other evidence of a close connection between the Semites and the continent of Africa as we can gather from the comments of other scholars. For example, George A. Barton, Professor of Semitic Languages, writes in THE JEWISH ENCYCLOPEDIA that "From Southern Arabia emigrants . . . established themselves in Africa. . . . These Semites are known as Ethiopians." [42] They came, as you will note from our earlier discussion, from the very direction of Israel and Havilah, the regions inhabited by the Cushite ancestors of Abraham and the Yoruba.

Without exploring other areas of Biblical and Middle East history, the preceding examples of the existence of an early or proto-Hebrew civilization under Abraham and their ultimate infusion into the blood culture of Black Africa, dating back to the eras of Moses and Solomon, should suffice to prove once and for all that the Black man is part of the parent stock which reaches back to the Original Israelites. The full extent of this ancient civilization is visible throughout Black Africa, not only in the quantity of the evidence, not merely as subsidiary or secondary influences, but as basic concepts which underlie the beliefs, practices and fabric of life in Black Africa.

(Below)   From: " *The Dark Continent's Royal Remnants,"*
TIME MAGAZINE, September 10, 1973:

THE OBA OF BENIN.   Benin's history was once the brightest of all the African kingdoms: its famous bronze sculptures are collector's items across the world. Today, 450,000 members of this Nigerian tribe are led by Oba Akenzua II, 74.

Chapter Eight

AFRICA IS THE HOMELAND OF JUDAISM, TOO!

MANY OF THE MOST IMPORTANT EVENTS to shape the nature and destiny of the *Hebraic and Judaic way of life* began in Africa. This cannot be said of any other major world religion. And these events, to the extent they underlie native Black African culture and beliefs, never left the African continent. Here are some of the reasons for this conclusion briefly summarized:

1. There is evidence in the Bible and elsewhere that Abraham, the Original *Hebrew and father of the Israelites,* was of Cushite or Black African descent.

2. Abraham first traveled to Africa where he received permission to settle in the Middle East land of Canaan.

3. Moses, in many respects the "founder" of *the Israelite way of life* as we know it today, was born in Africa, and therefore was an African.

4. The first Passover, which was the prelude to the exodus under the leadership of Moses, occurred in Africa.

5. The scene of the all-important Mosaic Revelation on Mount Sinai took place in the Sinai Peninsula, adjacent to continental Africa.

In addition, we already have seen the evidence that native African Hebrews who lived in Africa for many generations, settled Black Africa through their Ashanti, Fulani, Yoruba, Ethiopic, Bantu and other offspring, and today represent the majority of people living in these areas.

In conclusion, we can say that native Black African civilization is rooted in a Hebrew culture, as much at home in the soil of Africa and the hearts of Africans as in the Middle East. To be sure, it contains much that is alien and corrupted. However, no people, no culture, no society is without its admixture. It is a fact of life about which we may be *elated.* It is symbolic of the common brotherhood of mankind. But this does not negate the fact that most Black Americans descend from a "parent stock" which dates back to the earliest Hebrews.

Black Americans can *have a feeling of great elation* over their African-Israelite heritage. It has played a major role in shaping world history. And to the extent this ancestry is important to peoples of other races and colors, it reflects the full glory of a united humanity!

Chapter Nine

THE AFRICAN-ISRAELITES OF THE UNITED STATES

ROOTLESS! THIS ONE WORD describes the plight of the Black Man in America. Ruthlessly torn from his African home, the Black Man was cast into slavery and denied almost every semblance of his human dignity. He was considered a chattel, treated worse than an animal. After Emancipation, he was left homeless, illiterate, impoverished, politically powerless, and without a family or social structure on which to draw sustenance of any value except the most meager. He had nothing but alien cultural and spiritual substitutes to comfort him in his darkest hours of anguish.

The situation in Africa was not much better. Torn by years of inter-tribal warfare, which often pitted family against family, village against village, emasculated by colonialist and missionary intrigues and caprices, the Black African lost all but a glimmer of his ancient heritage. With the onslaughts of Christianity and Islam, even his native beliefs became diluted and lost beyond repair.

Our book, THE HEBREW HERITAGE OF BLACK AFRICA, tries to mend some of the damage that has been done. It is an attempt to provide the reader with some insights about the Black African heritage and its relationship to the mainstream of history.

There are many thousands of Black people in America, in the *Caribbean, in other parts of the Western Hemisphere,* and in Africa, who recognize *that* they are descendants of the

72

early Hebrews. There are over *300* congregations and other groups in this country alone, plus others in the Caribbean and Africa that testify to this fact.

Who are some of the pioneers for modern Black Israel in America? What have been the fruits of their efforts and travails? It is, of course, impossible to give credit to everyone; space does not permit it. Besides those whose names we know, there are many, many others who have departed our earthly world whose names and deeds are remembered only by their loved ones and the legacies which they left to succeeding generations.

PROPHET WILLIAM S. CROWDY was one such early pioneer. Born in St. Mary's County, Maryland, in 1847, he was discharged from the Army in 1872 after fighting in the Civil War. He founded the Beth El Temple Association of Prophetic Israelites in 1896, which is now the oldest and largest Israelite congregation in America. His successors include Rabbis Howard Zebulun Plummer and Levi Solomon Plummer. Presently, there are over 50 Beth El tabernacles in the United States alone, spanning from Alaska to Florida, and from New York to California. There are many more branches in the Caribbean and in South and Central Africa.

By 1915 there were approximately eight Israelite congregations in the New York City area. Black Hebrews came to this city of immigrants from Ethiopia and other parts of Africa, the West Indies, and, of course, from the South. Some early leaders include Rabbi Joshua Ford, Rabbi Albert Moses, Rabbi Israel ben Newman and Rabbi Wentworth Matthew, the latter, until his passing, leader of the Ethiopian Hebrew Congregation of Harlem. The area also is represented in part by the New York Federation of Israelite Rabbis, which includes Rabbi Eliezer Brooks, Rabbi Clifton Woods and Rabbi Yermiyahu ben Yisrael.

Chicago, too, is an important center of Black Israel. As a

result of the pioneering efforts of Rabbi Abihu Reuben and others, the United Leaders Council of Hebrew Israelites was founded to coordinate and promote the interests of the community. Before the High Holy Days, toward the end of the summer, the organization has sponsored a convention and parade. An article in THE CHICAGO DEFENDER (1973) estimated, "There are 12 to 15 separate Black Jewish congregations in Chicago, plus hundreds of small black Jewish groups." [1]

Philadelphia is another city which shares in the history of "Black Jews" in America. Besides Prophet Crowdy, who eventually settled here *in 1899*, some of the well-known names include Prophet F. S. Cherry, Rabbi Solomon Israel (Sherman Johnson), Prince George Kennedy, Rabbi Wallace Lyles, Bishop F. K. Murphy, and others.

Altogether there are congregations and other centers in such far-flung cities as Los Angeles, Norfolk, Jacksonville, Atlanta, Cleveland, Detroit, Baltimore, Cincinnati, Boston, Youngstown, Providence and elsewhere. There are also revitalized communities in the West Indies, Nigeria, East and South Africa, Ethiopia, and the State of Israel itself.

Besides their usual congregational activities, African-Israelite congregations have a program called "Reclamation." Similar in many respects to conversion, its purpose involves the reclaiming of the person's original African-Hebrew heritage through formal identification with the Israelite community and spirit.

Most Israelite congregations have their own schools where they teach the Torah (Bible) for its moral, cultural and spiritual insights, as well as African-Hebrew language, songs, dances, history and rituals. Emphasis is placed on education, good deeds (mitzvot), family life, manliness and an equal role for women. The major Hebrew holy days are observed, among them being Passover, Rosh Hashanah, Yom Kippur, and the weekly Sabbath. African-Israelite garb is worn at special gatherings and occasions and present a very colorful sight. Hebrew is taught in most congregations, and some have special courses in Ashanti, Yoruba and related African languages.

African-Israelites have their own schools of higher learning. There is the Israelite Rabbinical Seminary in Harlem. Beth El Temple has its own seminary in Virginia. The Yeshiva (religious school) founded by Rabbi Joseph Lazarus, another Israelite pioneer, ordains rabbis in Chicago. Some students attend predominantly White Jewish institutions such as Hebrew Union College-Jewish Institute of Religion, the Jewish Theological Seminary, and Yeshiva University, both at undergraduate and graduate levels. We also can add the Hebrew University in Jerusalem.

The African-Israelite community in America welcomes inquiries and has men and women who are willing and able to furnish answers and introduce you personally to the community, if this is your wish.

Chapter Ten

A SHORT REVIEW

WE HAVE PUT INTO QUESTION-AND-ANSWER form some of what we have discussed in the previous chapter of this book. It will help you to recall what you have read, and serves as a kind of review. The questions and their answers are not in order of importance. We think they are important to anyone who wishes to understand more about the Black Heritage and the history of Africa and the Middle East.

HISTORICAL PERSPECTIVE

Is there evidence of a Hebrew civilization in Black Africa, the ancestral home of most Black Americans? YES! Professor Joseph J. Williams of Boston College, who spent more than 11 years investigating, says, "The ancient Hebrews (are) parent stock from which the ancient Ashanti (and related West Africans) evolved." He adds, "It was the continuous influx of Hebrew settlers trekking up the Nile which eventually spread itself across Africa to the Niger River and thence pretty much the whole of West Africa."

What are some examples of Biblical Hebrew culture and religion in Black West Africa? HERE ARE SOME BASIC ONES: The word for God in Ashanti is "Yahweh," the same as in Hebrew. The Ashanti word for Creator is "Bore-bore," the same as in Hebrew. The Ashanti word for Law-giver is "Toro," almost identical to the Law-giving Torah of the *ancient Israelites*. Most West Africans (not influenced by Christianity or Islam) observe Saturday as their Sabbath, as *commanded in the Hebrew Scriptures* (commonly known as the Old Testament). The Ashanti priests wear a 12-part breast (*viz.* the twelve tribes of Israel) and a gold-emblem turban, both found together only among the Biblical priests of Israel. The Ashanti are typical of and inter-related to most Black West African peoples, and live today in Ghana, the very heart of the old slave coast.

Is there evidence of a Hebrew civilization elsewhere in Black Africa? YES! In virtually every country in Black Africa, remnants of an earlier Hebrew civilization can be found. Modern-day Ethiopians trace their ancestry to the ancient kingdom founded by Solomon and the Queen of Sheba (Makéda), with its capital at Gondar. The Yoruba of Nigeria have a historic tradition that they are descended from the Cushite followers of King Nimrod, and who, like the original Israelites, were forced to leave ancient Babylonia for the land of Israel.

Is there Biblical evidence of Hebrews living in Black Africa? YES! For example, the Prophet Isaiah, who lived about 725 B.C.E. (B.C.), said that God would recover the Israelites "from Cush," which is Ethiopia and the Sudanese Republic. The Prophet Zephaniah referred to Hebrews living "beyond the rivers of Ethiopia." This is confirmed by Leo Africanus, a 16th century explorer and historian, that Israelites at the time of Solomon lived between "Ethiopia and the Congo," the very heart of Black Africa.

Are Black Americans descendants of the "Original" Israelites? Black Hebrews trace their ancestry to Abraham, the Hebrew patriarch. He was born of a father, Terah, whom both Hebrew and Arabic traditions record was chief minister of King Nimrod, the Cushite ruler of ancient Babylonia about 2450 B.C.E. (B.C.). The Bible, in Genesis 2:11-13 gives to ancient Babylonia the name "Havilah," which the ENCYCLO-PEDIA AMERICANA says is a region "inhabited by the sons of Cush." Dr. George Cameron, an archeologist at the University of Chicago, confirms this with his own statement that there is "evidence that an early negroid population once extended along the shores of the Persian Gulf" in the exact region where Abraham was born. The Book of Daniel, which is part of the Bible and written in Babylonia, refers to the "Ancient of Days" whose hair was like "pure wool," a likely allusion to Abraham himself.

Who are White Jews, if the Black Man comes from the ancient Hebrews? There is considerable scholarly evidence that White Jews are largely the descendants of ancient Roman, Greek, Turkish, Armenian and other Caucasian groups, who adopted, or converted, to Judaism over the centuries. Importantly, historians agree the word "Semite" originally had a cultural meaning, not a racial one. Thus it was the culture of a person which determined whether he was Semitic in earlier times, not his color or race.

ASHANTI SAYINGS:

WOPE AKA ASEM AKYERE ONYANKO-PON A, KA KYERE MFRAMA -- "If you want to talk to God, tell it to the winds."

ONYAME NKRABEA MI KWATIBEA -- "The destiny God has assigned you, cannot be avoided."

BIBLIOGRAPHY

CHAPTER 1. *THE IMPORTANCE OF THIS BOOK*

1. WILLIAMS, JOSEPH J., *Hebrewisms of West Africa*, 1931, page 35
2. JOHNSTON, HARRY H., *The Negro In the New World*, 1910, page 27
3. WILLIAMS, page 93

CHAPTER 2. *THE BROADER SCENE*

CHAPTER 3. *THE ASHANTI OF WEST AFRICA*

1. WILLIAMS, JOSEPH J., *Hebrewisms of West Africa*, 1931, page 22
2. MANNIX, DANIEL, and COWLEY, MALCOLM, *Black Cargoes: A History of the Atlantic Slave Trade*, 1962, page 9
3. CHANTRE, ERNEST, *"Contribution a l'etude des races humaines de la Guinee, les Ashantis"* -- Bulletin, Societe d'Anthropolgie de Lyon, 1910, page 36
4. ARCIN, ANDRE, *La Guinee Francaise*, 1907, page 169
5. DIXON, ROLAND B., *Racial History of Man*, 1923, page 233
6. DIXON, page 233 ff.
7. BAUMANN, HERMANN, *The Division of Work According to Sex in Africa Hoe Culture,"* Journal of the International Institute of African Languages and Cultures, 1928, Volume I, page 301
8. NEWLAND, H. OSMAN, *West Africa*, 1922, page 94 (cf. CLARIDGE, WALTON W., *History of the Gold Coast and Ashanti*, 1915)
9. WILLIAMS, page 35
10. WILLIAMS, page 36

CHAPTER 4. *ASHANTI HEBREWISMS*

1. RATTRAY, R. SUTHERLAND, *Religion and Art in Ashanti*, 1927, page 28
2. CHRISTALLER, J. G., *Dictionary of the Asante and Fante Language*, 1881, pages 9, 561
3. DEAN, JOHN BATHURST, *The Worship of the Servant*, 1833, page 173

4. HOWEY, M. OLDFIELD, *The Encircled Serpent*, page 219

5. WILLIAMS, JOSEPH J., *Hebrewisms of West Africa*, 1931, page 45, footnotes 14, 15

6. DESPLAGNES, LOUIS, *La Plateau Central Nigerien*, 1907, page 106

7. WILLIAMS, page 61

8. LEVI, GERSON B., *"Ashan,"* Jewish Encyclopedia, 1902, Volume II, page 177

9. BROWN, DRIVER AND BRIGGS, *Hebrew and English Lexicon*, page 798

10. WILLIAMS, page 61

11. RATTRAY, *Ashanti Proverbs*, 1916, page 23

12. CHRISTALLER, page xix

13. RATTRAY, page 118

14. WILLIAMS, page 58, footnote 81

15. WILLIAMS, page 56 (cf. to RATTRAY, *Ashanti Proverbs*, page 32)

16. WILLIAMS, page 58

17. WILLIAMS, page 61

18. RATTRAY, *Religion and Art in Ashanti*, 1927, Chapter XXIX

19. WILLIAMS, page 61

20. RATTRAY, pages 79-81, 84-85

21. WILLIAMS, pages 62-63 (cf. URLIN, E. L., *A Short History of Marriage*, 1903, page 108 ff.)

22. RATTRAY, page 62

23. WILLIAMS, page 63 (cf. Leviticus 15:19-29)

CHAPTER 5. *THE SUPREME BEING OF THE ASHANTI*

1. MOORE, GEORGE FOOT, *Judaism in the First Centuries of the Christian Era*, 1927, Volume I, page 112

2. BLUNT, A. W. F., *Israel Before Christ*, 1924, page 72

3. OTTLEY, R. L., *A Short History of the Hebrews of the Roman Period*, 1923, page 102

4. VIGOUROUX, F., *Dictionnaire de la Bible*, 1895, Volume III, page 815

5. BOSMAN, WILLIAM, *A New and Accurate Description of the Coast of Guinea, Divided Into Gold, the Slave and the Ivory Coasts*, 1721, page 179 ff.

6. RATTRAY, R. SUTHERLAND, Ashanti, 1923, page 141

BIBLIOGRAPHY (Continued)

7. RATTRAY, page 141
8. ELLIS, ALFRED BURTON, *Tshi-Speaking Peoples of the Gold Coast of West Africa*, 1887, page 309; *The Yoruba-Speaking Peoples of the Slave Coast*, 1894, page 219
9. CHRISTALLER, J. G., *Dictionary of the Asante and Fante Language*, 1881, page 291
10. CLAY, ALBERT T., *The Empire of the Amorites*, 1919, page 54
11. CLAY, page 72
12. RATTRAY, *Ashanti Proverbs*, 1916, page 18
13. WILLIAMS, page 75, footnote 31
14. WILLIAMS, page 75, footnote 32
15. RATTRAY, *Ashanti*, page 294
16. BOSMAN, page 179 ff.
17. COOPER, DAVID L., *"The God of Israel,"* Messiah Series, 1968
18. CRUICKSHANK, BRODIE, *Eighteen Years On the Gold Coast of Africa*, Volume II, 1853 (cf. 1966 edition, page 126)
19. CRUICKSHANK (cf. 1966 edition, page 127, note)
20. ILLUSTRATED LONDON NEWS, Volume 64, February 14, 1874, page 144
21. ILLUSTRATED LONDON NEWS, page 143
22. ILLUSTRATED LONDON NEWS, Volume 64, February 7, 1874, page 126
23. STANLEY, HENRY MORTON, *Coomassie to Magdala*, 1874, page 126
24. STANLEY, DOROTHY, *Autobiography of Sir Henry Morton Stanley*, 1909, page 291
25. STANLEY, HENRY MORTON, page 126
26. ELLIS, A. B., *The Land of the Fetish*, 1883, page 221
27. WILLIAMS, page 82
28. BOWDITCH, T. EDWARD, *Mission From Cape Coast Castle to Ashantee*, 1819, page 229
29. STANLEY, page 131
30. RATZEL, FRIEDRICH, *History of Mankind*, 1886, Volume III, page 129
31. WILLIAMS, page 82
32. HIRSCH, EMIL G., *"High Priest,"* Jewish Encyclopedia, Volume 6, 1902, page 390
33. RATTRAY, page 282, footnote 5
34. WILLIAMS, page 83, footnote 71
35. RATTRAY, page 263

36. WILLIAMS, page 83
37. JUNIOR JUNIOR ENCYCLOPEDIA, *"Torah,"* page 316
38. WILLIAMS, pages 90, 91

CHAPTER 6. *OTHER HEBREWISMS IN BLACK AFRICA*

1. SLOUSCHZ, NAHUM, *Travels in North Africa*, 1927, page 430
2. WILSON, J. LEIGHTON, *Western Africa: Its History, Condition and Prospects*, 1856, page iv
3. WILSON, pages 216, 220 ff.
4. WILSON, page 220 ff.
5. BOSMAN, WILLIAM, *A New Accurate Description of the Guinea Coast*, 1721, page 125
6. BOSMAN, page 180
7. PARK, MUNGO, *Travels In the Interior Districts of Africa*, 1810, page 116
8. PARKC, page 406 (cf. Job 31:26 ff.)
9. KOHLER, KAUFMAN, *"New Moon,"* Jewish Encyclopedia, Volume 9, 1902, page 243
10. WILLIAMS, JOSEPH J., *Africa's Gods*, Anthropological Series of the Boston Graduate School, Series 2 (Dahomey), June, 1936, page 161
11. HERSKOVITZ, MELVILLE, J., *An Outline of Dahomean Religious Beliefs*, 1933, Number 41, page 22 ff.
12. HERSKOVITZ, page 77
13. SKETCHERLY, J. A., *Dahomey As It Is*, 1874, page 461
14. HERMAN, AUGUSTE, *A Travers le Pays Ewe*, Echo des Missions Africaines de lyon, T.XXVIII (1929), page 81 ff.
15. HERMAN, page 81 ff.
16. WILLIAMS, page 167
17. BURTON, RICHARD, *A Mission To Gilele, King of Dahomey*, 1864 (cf. 1966 edition, page 58, note 3)
18. ATKINS, JOHN, *A Voyage to Guinea*, 1735, page 168
19. LO BAGOLA, *Bata Kindai Amgoza, An African Savage's Own Story*, 1930, pages 42 ff. (cf. Lo Bagola, *"An African Savage's Own Story,"* Scribner's, March-June, 1929
20. KREPPFL, J., *Juden und Judentum von Heute*, 1926, page 807
21. BOUCHE, PIERRE, *La Cote des Enclaves et Le Dohomey*, 1885, page 268
22. BOUCHE, page 268

23. REINDORF, CARL CHRISTIAN, *History of the Gold Coast Asante*, 1895, page 6
24. BASDEN, G. T., *Among the Ibo of Nigeria*, 1921, page 31
25. BASDEN, page 215
26. COLLINS, ROBERT, *African Encounter; A Doctor in Nigeria*, 1960, page 198
27. COHEN, GERSON D., *Great Ages and Ideas of the Jewish People*
28. MOREL, EDMUND D., *Affairs of West Africa*, 1902, page 140
29. MOREL, page 148
30. ABADIE, MAURICE, *La Colonie du Niger*, 1927, page 184 ff.
31. ABADIE, page 184 ff.
32. WILLIAMS, JOSEPH J., *Hebrewisms of West Africa*, 1931, page 249
33. MOREL, page 148 ff.
34. MOREL, page 148 ff.
35. MOREL, page 151
36. WARD, HERBERT, *A Voice From the Congo*, 1910, page 252
37. SUMNER, W. G., KELLER, A. G. and DAVIE, *The Science of Society*, Volume III, 1927, pages 868, 870, 899, 907
38. ENNIS, W. MERLIN, *The Ovimbundu*, Copy of H.C.C. Library, MS Number 2103 (cf. WILLIAMS, JOSEPH J., *Af-rica's Gods, Series 3 (Congo and Angola)*, June, 1937, page 99)
39. RATZEL, FRIEDRICH, *History of Mankind*, 1896, Volume III, page 134
40. CLARKE, JOHN, *Specimens of Dialects: Short Vocabularies of Languages: and Notes of Countries and Customs in Africa*, 1848, page 91
41. CIATTI, GIUSEPPE, *The Agekoyo of Kenya*, H.C.C. Library, MS Number 2025 (cf. WILLIAMS, JOSEPH J., *Africa's Gods, Series 4 (East Africa)*, December, 1937, page 191
42. CIATTI (cf. WILLIAMS, pages 191-193)

CHAPTER 7. *AFRICAN HEBREWS: THE OFFSPRING OF ABRAHAM*

1. MERCER, SAMUEL A. B., *Extra-Biblical Sources for Hebrew and Jewish History*, 1913, page 9
2. MERCER, page 9, notes
3. ORLINSKY, HARRY M., "Moses," B'nai B'rith Great Books, Series 1, pages 11-12
4. WILLIAMS, JOSEPH J., *Hebrewisms of West Africa*, 1931, p. 258

BIBLIOGRAPHY (Continued)

5. MENDELSSOHN, SIDNEY, *The Jews in Africa*, 1920, page 2
6. FLEG, EDMOND, *The Life of Moses*, 1928, page 56 ff.
7. MOREL, EDMOND D., *Affairs of West Africa*, 1902, page 151
8. WILLIAMS, page 267
9. SEE CHAPTER 3
10. TELLEZ, F. BALTHAZAR, *Travels of the Jesuits in Ethiopia*, 1710
11. MENDELSSOHN, page 5 ff.
12. PLOWDEN, WALTER C., *Travels in Abyssinia and Galla Country*, 1868
13. MORIE, LOUIS J., *Historie de l'Ethiopie*, 1904, Vol. II, page 94
14. LUDOLPHI, JOB, *Historia Aethiopica*, 1681, Volume I, Chapter XVI, #46
15. BARTON, GEORGE A., *"Falasha,"* Jewish Encyclopedia, 1905, Volume II, page 186
16. ISAIAH 11:11
17. ZEPHANIAH 3:10
18. AFRICANUS, JOHN LEO, *A Geographical History of Africa*, translated by PRORY, JOHN, 1600, page 379
19. DIXON, ROLAND B., *Racial History of Man*, 1923, page 233 ff.
20. See Chapter 3
21. KAUTSKY, KARL, *Are the Jews a Race?*, 1926, page 118
22. KAUTSKY, *Foundations of Christianity*, 1925, page 261 ff.
23. TAYLOR, GRIFITH, *Environment and Race*, 1927, page 184 ff.
24. PITTARD, EUGENE, *Race and History*, 1926, page 350 ff.
25. *"Nimrod,"* Encyclopedia Americana, 1965, Volume 20, page 356
26. MULLER, MAX W., *"Cush,"* Jewish Encyclopedia, Volume 5, page 258
27. THE COLUMBIA LIPPINCOTT GAZETTEER OF THE WORLD, 1966, page 64
28. THE NEW COLUMBIA ENCYCLOPEDIA, 1975, page 95
29. *"Havilah,"* Encyclopedia Americana, page 766
30. SAYCE, A. H., *The Races of the Old Testament*, 1925, pages 102, 103
31. CAMERON, GEORGE C., *History of Early Iran*, 1968, page 17
32. JOHNSTON, HARRY H., *The Negro in the New World*, 1910, page 27, note 1
33. SELIGSOHN, MAX, *"Nimrod,"* Jewish Encyclopedia, 1905, Volume 9, page 309 (cf. Babylonian Talmud: Sefer ha-Yashar)

34. SELIGSOHN, page 309
35. SAYCE, A. H., *"Havilah,"* Jewish Encyclopedia, Volume 6, page 266
36. KROEBER, ALFRED LOUIS, *Anthropology,* 1923, page 450
37. CAMERON, page 51
38. GODBEY, ALLEN H., *The Lost Tribes a Myth: Suggestions Towards Rewriting Hebrew History,* 1930, page 155
39. *The Biblical World: A Dictionary of Biblical Archeology,* 1966, page 219
40. ARNETT, E. J., *The Rise of the Sokoto Fulani,* 1929, page 16 (translation of Bello, Muhammed Infaq al-Maysur, circa 1837)
41. DAVIDSON, BASIL, *A History of West Africa to the Nineteenth Century,* 1966, pages 101, 146, 184 (cf. original edition: *The Growth of African Civilization, West Africa 1000-1800*)
42. BARTON, GEORGE A., *"Falasha,"* Jewish Encyclopedia, Volume II, page 186

CHAPTER 8. *AFRICA IS THE HOMELAND OF JUDAISM, TOO!*

CHAPTER 9. *THE AFRICAN ISRAELITES OF THE U.S.*

1. MCCLORY, ROBERT, Chicago Defender, March 10, 1973, page 28

CHAPTER 10. *A SHORT REVIEW*

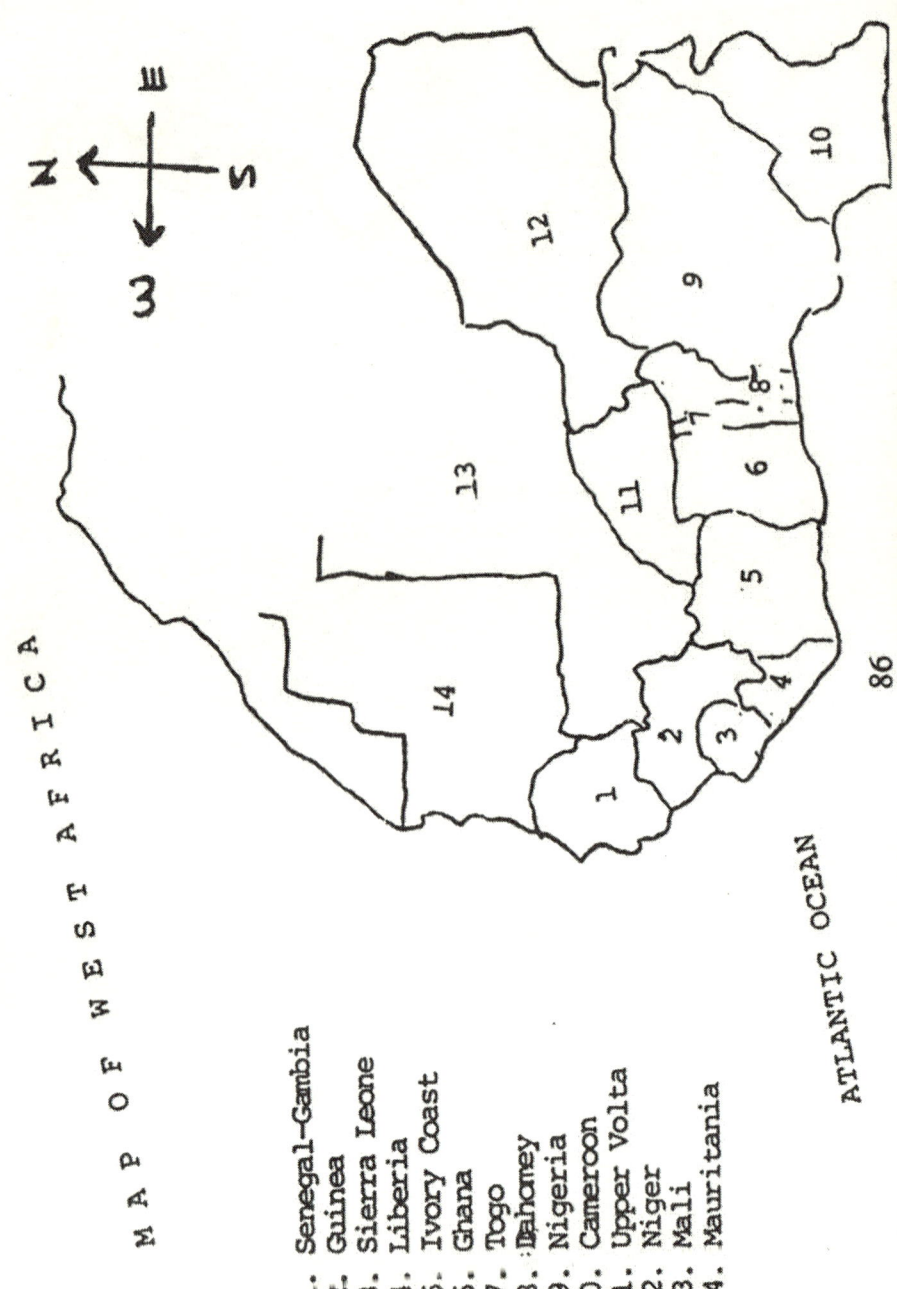

MAP OF WEST AFRICA

1. Senegal-Gambia
2. Guinea
3. Sierra Leone
4. Liberia
5. Ivory Coast
6. Ghana
7. Togo
8. Dahomey
9. Nigeria
10. Cameroon
11. Upper Volta
12. Niger
13. Mali
14. Mauritania

ATLANTIC OCEAN

86

PART II

Chapter 11

ABRAHAM, THE FRIEND OF GOD

THE GREATNESS OF THE MAN ABRAHAM, as outlined in the text of the Bible (in both the Hebrew Scriptures and, to a lesser degree, in the Greek Scriptures), is too often over-looked. Within spiritual and historical circles, how many times within a year do you hear a sermon, lecture or dis-cussion with God's revelation to Abraham as the topic? The answer is probably, "seldom, if ever." Yet, according to his life as recorded in the Book of Genesis and the testimonies of righteous prophets and kings succeeding him, Abraham is in a class all by himself.

Born "ÄV-RÄM" (*exalted father*) in circa 2056 B.C.E. (B.C.) in Ur, Babylonia (Ur of the Chaldees; pronounced *"oor"* and *"căldees"*), his father's name was Terah. This country was settled by Nimrod, son of Cush and grandson of Noah, in circa 2218 B.C.E. The land of "Cush" was to be renamed "Ethiopia" many centuries later by the Greeks. Abraham the Babylonian was, therefore, born in a land inhabited totally by Black people, whom he resembled.

Before we begin to discuss the spiritual greatness of the man who went on to become the God-fearing father of a mul-titude of nations, it must be pointed out that Abram was born into idolatrous surroundings, and his father, according to history, was an idol-maker. Aside from the Bible, the fol-lowing legend also supports the fact that idolatry was preva-lent in Babylonia where Abram was born:

89

Mankind descending from Adam became hopelessly corrupt and was swept away by the Deluge [Flood]. Noah alone was spared. But before many generations pass away, mankind once again becomes arrogant and impious, and moral darkness overspreads the earth. 'And God said, Let Abraham be — and there was light,' is the profound saying of the sages. In many a beautiful legend, it has been recounted how Abraham refused to walk in the way of the Tower-builders, and broke away from the debasing heathenisms of his contemporaries. In his early childhood one night, he looked at the stars under the clear Babylonian sky, and felt, 'These are the gods!' But the dawn came, and soon the stars could be seen no longer when the sun rose. 'This is my god, him will I adore!' he exclaimed. But then the sun set, and he hailed the moon as his deity. When in turn the moon was obscured, he cried out: 'This, too, is no god! There must be One who is the Maker of Sun, Moon and Stars.' Having gradually reached the momentous conviction that the Universe is the work of One Supreme Being who is the God of righteousness, he endeavors to open the eyes of others to the folly of idol-worship, and becomes the Preacher of the True Faith. In his father's house, the legend continues, there stood one great idol and a large number of smaller ones. Abraham broke all the smaller ones and then placed the hammer in the hand of the big idol. 'They quarreled among themselves,' he later explained to his dumb-founded father, 'and the big one thereupon took a hammer and shattered them all. Behold, it is still in his hands!' 'But there is no life and power in them to do such things,' his father answered in rage. 'Why, then, dost thou serve them? Can they hear thy prayers when thou callest upon them?' was the reply. Abraham was thereupon haled before the ruler of Babylon, Nimrod, who cast him into a fiery furnace (whence the name of the city 'Ur', which means <u>fire</u>). An angel of God rescues him unhurt from its devouring flames. Abraham the idol-wrecker is the father of that People which was to shatter all idolatries; which was to suffer all things, endure all things, and survive all things. The call of Abraham (Gen. ch. 12) is the beginning of the higher spiritual life of humanity.

After the marriage of Abram to Sarai, they, together with

Lot and Terah, journeyed toward Canaan, another land peopled totally by Blacks, as the man Canaan was a son of Ham. But before entering Canaan, they dwelled in Haran for a long season. During their sojourn there, many, many births took place and much material substance was acquired. It was in Haran that Abram's father, Terah, died.

THE SCENE CHANGES: "THE CALL OF ABRAM" BY EL SHADDAI (Almighty God)

The twelfth chapter of Genesis gives a vivid description of the "Call of Abraham" by the Almighty, and His instructions to leave the City of Haran and enter into Canaan. In Genesis 12:1-5, we find recorded:

> *"Now the LORD had said unto Abram, Get thee out from thy kindred, and from thy father's house, unto a land that I will show thee: And I will make of thee a great nation, and I will bless thee, and make thy name great; and thou shalt be a blessing; And I will bless them that bless thee, and curse him that curseth thee: and in thee shall all families of the earth be blessed. So Abram departed, as the LORD had spoken unto him; and Lot went with him: and Abram was seventy and five years old when he departed from Haran. And Abram took Sarai his wife, and Lot his brother's son, and all their substance that they had gathered, and the souls that they had gotten in Haran: and they went forth to go into the land of Canaan; and into the land of Canaan they came."*

God promised Abram that he would give his seed the land of Canaan; "there he *built* an altar unto the LORD, who appeared unto him" (Gen. 12:7). He then traveled in the area, observing the customs and traditions of the Canaanites, though not embracing them. He passed through Sichem and Moreh. Settling on a mountain, with Bethel on the west and Hai on the east, he again "*built* an altar unto the LORD, and called upon [*prayed in*] the name of the LORD."

Famine struck the land of his abode, and for the sake of survival he and his household journeyed to Egypt. Upon entering he made an agreement with his beautiful wife Sarai to say *"I am his sister"* to Pharoah, whom Abram had thought would take her and kill him. The king did take Sarai into his house, thus separating them, yet treating Abram well for her sake. According to what is recorded in Gen. 12:17, God plagued Pharoah and his house with great plagues, thus causing him to return her to Abram.

The greatness of Abram is manifested more and more by the many, many times that the God Most High revealed Himself to him; by his total obedience to the will of God; by being the only one throughout the entire scriptures -- Old Testament and New -- that God called "My friend"; by issuing a peaceful solution to the strife between his and Lot's herdsmen, and by maintaining the distinction of being commanded by the Creator to "Walk before Me, and be thou perfect." Furthermore, Abraham's belief and trust in the Almighty was of such nobility that Torah records of him:

"And he believed in the LORD; and He counted it to him for righteousness" (Gen. 15:6).

We are compelled to note here, however, that it was not a "rocking chair belief and trust" which Abram possessed, but an obedient, working one, which stirred him to follow every command of the Eternal One. The Only and All-wise God, apparently so impressed with the spirit and life of Abram, rewarded him a change of name, saying,

"As for Me, behold My covenant is with thee, and thou shalt be a father of many nations. Neither shall thy name any more be called Abram, but thy name shall be Abraham; for a father of many nations have I made thee" (Gen. 17:4-5).

(Abram means "*exalted father*"; Abraham means "*father of a multitude of nations.*")

Later, we find Abraham entering Gerer of Canaan. Upon arriving, King Abimelech took Sarah into his house; Abraham had already, once again, entered into a "say thou art my sister" agreement with her, as he had done in the case of the Pharoah. Being warned by God in a dream that Sarah was Abraham's wife, the king returned her to him. This portion of Abraham's life is told here to bring to light the important fact that Abraham has the distinction of being the first person in all of scripture to be called by God "a Prophet." The Lord's warning to Abimelech was, "Now therefore restore the man his wife; for he is a prophet, and he shall pray for thee . . ." (Gen. 20:7). This is not to say that prophets did not exist before Abraham, such as Noah and others, but that Abraham was the first to be specifically so designated.

Abraham's oldest son Ishmael, by Hagar, was blessed by the Almighty God, and was promised by Him to become fruitful and exceeding multitudinous. The Most High said further concerning Ishmael,

"Twelve princes shall he beget, and I will make him a great nation" (17:20).

Concerning Isaac, Abraham's second son, God made this promise:

"Sarah thy wife shall bear thee a son indeed; and thou shalt call his name Isaac; and I will establish My covenant with him for an everlasting covenant, and with his seed after him" (17:19).

Abraham's Faith Put to the Test

The Divine Being probably thought to Himself, "Abraham has obeyed me in all things which I have commanded him: (1) He left the idols of his father's house; (2) he has journeyed to Canaan; (3) he has circumcised the males of his house; (4) he has looked east, west, north, south, up and down; (5) he has walked before Me and been perfect; (6) he has paid his tithes, and (7) he has commanded his children and his household after him. I will now put him to the ultimate test":

> *"And He said, Take now thy son, thine only son Isaac, whom thou lovest, and get thee into the land of Moriah; and offer him there for a burnt offering upon one of the mountains which I will tell thee of."*

Abraham may not have found the command to have been too extraordinary, as child sacrifice was rife among the inhabitants of the lands of his many migrations. Consequently, without hesitation, he, accompanied by Isaac, made his way to Mount Moriah to carry out the command of his LORD. Isaac had ofttimes seen his father offer sacrifices, and he was fully acquainted with the necessary paraphernalia. Beholding the wood, fire and knife, Isaac discerned that there was something missing; and that was the lamb for the sacrifice. When he asked his father, "Where is the lamb for the burnt offering?," Abraham replied, "My son, God will provide Himself a lamb for a burnt offering." Laden with the necessary equipment, Abraham arrived at the site, built an altar, and proceeded to execute the Divine order.

> *". . . Abraham laid the wood in order, and bound Isaac his son, and laid him on the altar upon the wood. And Abraham stretched forth his hand, and took the knife to slay his son. And the angel of the LORD called unto him out of heaven, and said, Abraham, Abraham: and he said, Here am I. And he said, Lay not thine hand upon the lad, neither do thou any thing unto him: for now I know that thou fearest God, seeing thou hast not withheld thy son, thine only son from Me. And Abraham lifted up his eyes, and looked, and behold behind him a ram caught in a thicket by his horns; and Abraham went and took the ram, and offered him up for a burnt offering in the stead of his son"* (22:9-13).

Abraham called the name of the place of the sacrifice *"Jehovah-jireh"* (in Hebrew, *"Adonai-jireh"*) -- that is, "THE LORD WILL PROVIDE." I am a living witness to the fact that it is <u>still</u> true today: "THE LORD <u>WILL</u> PROVIDE!"

From this and other Biblical accounts we know that God is against human sacrifice, and we are disallowed to believe that the Most High would offer up someone to die for the sins of the trillions of people who have lived since the beginning of Man, the more than six billion of the earth's present inhabitants, and the probable trillions who are yet unborn. (See the chapter, *"Did Ancient Israel's Animal Sacrificial System Prefigure the Crucifixion of Jesus?,"* on page 129 in my book entitled "A NON-CHRISTIAN'S RESPONSE TO CHRISTIANITY.")

We are inclined to conclude that the Divine command for Abraham to offer up his son and the *"voice from heaven"* which restrained him from doing so were not literal voices from the skies heard with the natural ear. God speaks to the hearts and minds of men and women from within, through other people, and by way of dreams, visions and signs.

Not only is Abraham heralded in the Hebrew Scriptures (O.T.) as "God's friend" (Isaiah 41:8), but in II Chron. 20:7 he is called "God's friend forever." Throughout the Biblical era men prayed in the name of the God of Abraham, and even today millions still do. Jesus often gave credence to Abraham in his teaching (Matt. 3:9, John 8:39, 56, et al). Apostles James, Paul and other contributors to the Greek Scriptures (N.T.) in their various epistles and speeches also attribute greatness to the Father of the Faithful.

The Most High was so well-pleased with the life of Father Abraham, that when He identified Himself to the children of Israel in Egypt, He said to Moses:

> *"Thus shalt thou say to the children of Israel, The LORD God of your fathers, <u>the God of Abraham,</u> the God of Isaac, and the God of Jacob, hath sent me unto you: <u>this</u>*

is My name forever, and this is My memorial unto all generations" (Exodus 3:15).

Seven years after the death of Sarah, Abraham married Keturah, and she bore him six sons, the most noted of which today is Midian, the father of the Midianites. Abraham lived to see children born to those six sons.

The life of Abraham closes in circa 1822 B.C.E. (B.C.), and the Book of Genesis, from the Hebrew Version of the Scriptures, gives us this account of his death:

> *"And these are the days of the years of Abraham's life which he lived, a hundred threescore and fifteen [175] years. And Abraham expired, and died in a good old age, an old man, and full of years; and was gathered to his people."*

GOD'S PROMISE TO ABRAHAM IN GENESIS 12:3 and 22:18 –

". . . And in thee [Abraham] and in thy seed shall all families of the earth be blessed."

WHAT WAS ONE MAJOR WAY IN WHICH THIS PROMISE WAS FULFILLED?

We could not possibly close the chapter on the life of Abraham without discussing the very first promise which the Almighty made to him and detailing how its fulfillment has been for the salvation of the world.

With the destruction of Jerusalem in A.D. 70 by Titus and the Roman Army, thousands of Black Israelites of that era migrated through flight to western and southern Africa. Their posterity remained there for nearly 1,400 years, continued the practice of their Hebraic tenets, were caught up in the West African Slave Trade of the 14th, 15th, 16th and 17th centuries -- along with many African tribes -- and enslaved in the Western Hemisphere. (All this and more has been thoroughly documented in the first portion of this book. For further documentation, read Rudolph Windsor's *"From Babylon To Timbuktu"* and Professor Joseph J. Williams' *"The Hebrew-isms of West Africa."*)

These descendants of the Hebrew-Israelite patriarchs -- Abraham, Isaac and Jacob -- have been and still are a blessing to the world in many ways. The buying, selling and enslavement of Black flesh from 1517 to 1865 went unchallenged, and scores of countries and thousands of slave-traders became filthy rich in the process. The trillions of dollars profited from the enslavement and the abominable treatment of tens of millions of Africans by America, Portugal, Spain, France, England, South America, Central America, and the Caribbean have contributed in a major way to many natons today being the wealthiest on planet earth.

After 1808 -- the last year that Africans were <u>supposed</u> to be exported -- Slavery still lasted another 57 years, ending in 1865. This brought the total number of years of slave-trading and formal Slavery to 348. Each of those African victims had a life-time job, but not one of them ever had a pay day. **The lucrative Slave Trade, Slavery, and Free Slave Labor during those 348 years have to a great degree built many countries, both structurally and financially. What a blessing the descendants of Abraham, Isaac and Jacob -- as well as the other millions from Africa who survived the Middle Passage -- have been to the world!** With the countries involved in Slavery sharing their wealth with the countries not involved, through commerce and monetary gifts, they, too, have become benefactors of the Slave Trade. The wealth accumulated over the span of those three and a half centuries has been passed down from generation to generation, and the children of those slavetraders and masters still bask today in the riches acquired by their ancestors. Termed by some as *"old money,"* it is better defined as *"Blood Money"*! The Black race has made the supreme sacrifice, and has thus become the Saviour (salvation) of the world, through the Infinite Wisdom and Will of the Creator. We are clay in the Potter's hand; for the Most High has declared, *"Behold, I have refined thee, but not as silver; I have tried thee in the furnace of affliction"* (Isaiah 48:10, Hebrew version). Do not despair; WE AS A PEOPLE WILL ONE DAY GET TO THE PROMISED LAND!

Have you ever given thought as to where this nation and many others would be on the economic scale were it not for Institutionalized Slavery? The Bible records how the enslaved ancient Israelites built for Pharoah the treasure cities of Pithom and Rameses (Ex. 1:11). For more than four centuries now, the enslaved descendants of those Israelites have built treasure cities, including the laying of thousands of miles of railroads, here in America (the second Egypt) -- such cities as New York, Chicago, Philadelphia, Atlanta, Richmond, Baltimore, Wilmington, and Birmingham, just to name a few.

Truly, the promise of Genesis 12:3 and 22:18 has been fulfilled many times over -- the Most High's promise which proclaims that *"In thee* [Abraham, Isaac and Jacob] *and in thy seed shall all families and nations of the earth be blessed."* (The exact same promises are made by the Almighty to Isaac, in Gen. 26:4, and to Jacob, in Gen. 28:14.)

Abraham goes down in the annals of Biblical history as one of the greatest men of all time. There is no record of his having parted the sea like Moses; divided the Jordan like Joshua; healed the sick like Isaiah; raised the dead like Elijah; caused iron to swim like Elisha, or given sight to the blind like Jesus. Yet, he is the chief patriarch of the Israelite people; the exhibitor of excellent hospitality to the three men of God who met him in the plains of Mamre; received the promise from Almighty God Himself that his seed would be as the stars of heaven for multitude and as the sand upon the sea-shore innumerable; walked before his Maker, and was perfect; was recipient from God of the guarantee that kings and nations would come out of him; was willing to slay his son as a burnt offering to his Creator, and remains to this day the father of a multitude of nations. But more important than all of the foregoing is the fact that the man Abraham IS THE FRIEND OF GOD, EVEN GOD'S FRIEND FOREVER!

> *"AND ABRAM* [Abraham] *WAS VERY RICH IN CATTLE, IN SILVER, AND IN GOLD"* (Gen. 13:2).

BEWARE OF MEMBERS OF THE CHURCH OF LATTER DAY SAINTS -- THE MORMONS -- WHO ARE TRYING ON A VERY LARGE SCALE TO RECRUIT AFRICAN AMERICANS AS MEMBERS. MANY ARE TOO YOUNG TO REMEMBER THAT JUST A FEW YEARS AGO IT WAS THE POLICY OF THE MORMON CHURCH THAT PEOPLE OF AFRICAN ANCESTRY COULD NOT BE MINISTERS OR CHOIR MEMBERS OF THEIR CHURCH. THEY TAUGHT THAT THE BLACK RACE WAS THE CURSE OF HAM, AND WAS ORDAINED BY GOD TO BE HEWERS OF WOOD AND DRAWERS OF WATER. NOW THE MORMONS ARE IN THE BLACK COM-MUNITY PROSELYTIZING MEMBERS OF OUR RACE. BEWARE!

"The Bible: How Readest Thou?"

It is one thing to read the Bible through,
Another thing to read to learn and do;
Some read it with design to learn to read,
But to the subject pay but little heed.
Some read it as their duty once a week,
But no instruction from the Bible seek;
While others read it with but little care,
With no regard to how they read nor where.
Some read it as a history to know
How people lived three thousand years ago.
Some read to bring themselves into repute,
By showing others how they can dispute;
While others read because their neighbors do,
To see how long 'twill take to read it through.
Some read it for the wonders that are there,
How David killed a lion and a bear;
While others read it with uncommon care,
Hoping to find some contradiction there!
Some read as though it did not speak to them,
But to the people at Jerusalem.
One reads it as a book of mysteries,
And won't believe the very thing he sees.
One reads with father's specks upon his head,
And sees the thing just as his father said.

Some read to prove a pre-adopted creed —
Hence understand but little that they read,
For every passage in the book they bend
To make it suit that all important end!
Some people read as I have often thought:
To teach the book instead of being taught;
And some there are who read it out of spite —
I fear there are but few who read it right.
So many people in these latter days
Have read the Bible in so many ways,
That few can tell which system is the best,
For every party contradicts the rest!
But read it prayerfully, and you will see,
Although men contradict, God's words agree.
For what the early Bible prophets wrote,
We find that Christ and his apostles quote.

– AUTHOR UNKNOWN

Chapter 11

IT'S ALL THE FAULT
OF ADAM
(An Old Nigerian Folk Tale)

MANY YEARS AGO there lived in a small village in Nigeria a poor man. This man was so impoverished, that the sight of him would almost make one break down in tears. Rather than give up on life, he found an old wheel barrow on the junk pile, repaired it, and began his struggle to merely survive. He went throughout his little village selling fire wood and heralding this slogan over and over again as he went on his way: *"Wood, good wood, very good wood; it's all the fault of Adam!"*

The king of Nigeria decided to take a trip through the small village to see if the report he had heard of this poverty-stricken area was altogether true. So he ordered that his chariot be made ready for the journey. As he entered the village and began riding through and observing the conditions, he noticed in particular this poor man clad in tattered clothes and pushing his rusty, wobbly wheel barrow, crying out, *"Wood, good wood, very good wood; it's all the fault of Adam!"*

The king commanded his driver to stop the chariot. He descended from his lofty position, went over to the poor man and said, "Sell me a bundle of your wood." The man was astonished in seeing one arrayed in such finery and accompanied by a horseman and chariot approach him for a meager bundle of wood. Not only did the king purchase the bundle of wood, but he said to the poor man, "Your destitute condition and your cry of 'Wood, good wood, very good wood; it's all the fault of Adam,' has touched my heart. You should not have to suffer this way for what another man has done. Come with me just as you are, and I will take you into my palace, for I am the king of Nigeria."

The poor man immediately left the rest of his wood and his wheel barrow on the side of the road and followed the king to his chariot. Upon reaching the palace, the king welcomed him in and gave orders to his servants that he be bathed, shaved and given clean attire befitting one residing at the king's domain.

The man was then welcomed into the presence of the king, who said within the hearing of all the royal court, "HAIL TO ALL! MEET THE MAN WHOM I AM ADOPTING AS MY BROTHER. He has suffered much, but now his life is to be made sweet.

After six months had passed, the king decided to take a trip to a far country. He said to his new 'brother,' "I am going away for many days, and am leaving you in complete charge of the palace and all of its affairs. Should you need any assistance, I have given orders to the other subjects of the royal court to render you aid. The entire palace is yours to enjoy, only there is **one** restriction: DO NOT EVER, EVER GO INTO THE ROOM WITH THE GREEN DOOR! IS THAT UNDERSTOOD?" "Yes, sir, my lord," replied his 'brother.' The king then took his journey.

After a few days the king's brother began to stroll the palace with an aire of importance, drinking the best of the king's wine and faring sumptuously every day. Twice a day he changed into long, flowing robes and ate the best of all the foods. Servants in abundance and women, wine and song were at his beck and call around the clock. In fact, he began gaining so much weight that he had become sloppy and had begun stumbling over his long robes.

Day after day he strolled throughout the palace. And finally, he passed by the room with the green door. He casually looked at the door and kept strolling. Upon his second round through the palace, he came to the green door again. This time when he reached it he turned and faced the door for about seven seconds, then turned and walked away.

Two weeks went by, and the king's brother kept turning the king's command over and over in his mind: "DO NOT EVER, EVER GO INTO THE ROOM WITH THE GREEN DOOR!"

He began his usual walk through the kingly domain again at the beginning of a new week. This time upon reaching the green door he stared at it for a longer period of time and even touched it. The suspense was tearing him apart as he wondered just why he was not allowed to go inside the room with the green door, whereas all the other rooms of the mansion were available to him. He decided to leave the area and think it over, playing the mind game of 'shall I or shall I not?' Finally, he decided to go once again to the green door. This time upon arriving he frightfully touched the door knob, and the green door opened.

While he was in the green room the king just happened to return from his long trip. He asked for his brother, and no one seemed to know of his whereabouts, the palace was so immense. The king himself then went looking throughout for his brother. At last he went to the room with the green door, and there he found his brother examing the contents of the room.

When their eyes met, the king's brother said, "O my lord, my master, what have I done! I am so sorry!"

There was nothing in the room except the poor man's old tattered clothes and the bundle of wood that the king had bought from him, both tied together in one pack, sitting on the floor in a corner of the room. The man stood tremblingly afraid, not knowing what the king would say or do.

The king said to the man, "I picked you up and gave you a new life of ease and luxury, and entrusted to you the complete charge of my palace. I only ordered you not to go into the room with the green door. Now because you have disobeyed my command and have entered the room, I now sentence you back to your village and out into the streets with your old clothes and this bundle of wood.

So the man, no longer the king's brother, left the realm of the king and went back to his village at the king's word. He walked the streets for many more years thereafter, crying, *"Wood, good wood, very good wood!"* BUT NEVER AGAIN DID HE <u>EVER</u> SAY, *IT'S ALL THE FAULT OF ADAM!*

WE HAVE OURSELVES, AND ONLY OURSELVES, TO BLAME!

EXCUSES ARE TOOLS OF INCOMPETENCE, USED TO BUILD MONUMENTS OF NOTHINGNESS; AND THOSE WHO ENGAGE IN THEM SELDOM AMOUNT TO ANYTHING ELSE!

Chapter 12

FROM **ABRAHAM**
TO **DAVID** TO **JESUS:**
Their Ethnicity

The frail, pallid Christ depicted by artists in Christendom in contrast with a portrayal of Jesus based on Bible accounts

Sketch on left is what Michaelangelo and other European artists say that Jesus looked like. Sketch on right is what the Jehovah's Witnesses' *Awake Magazine* **of Dec. 8, 1998, says Jesus looked like. Are the JWs deceiving the public and millions of their Black members into believing that Jesus was Caucasian? Nowhere in the Bible does it say that Jesus looked like whom they depict here.**

IT HAS ALREADY BEEN UNDENIABLY ESTABLISHED in chapters 1-10 of this book and in the chapter entitled ABRAHAM, THE FRIEND OF GOD (page 89), that Abraham was of Shemitic-Hamitic origin; descended from a Shemite father, Terah; born in Babylonia, a country settled by the Hamitic Nimrod, and assigned by God the letters -'h-a-m' at the end of his name, which signifies a Hamitic connection.

The genealogy recorded in Matthew 1:1 reads, "The book of the generation of Jesus Christ, the son of David, the son of Abraham." Verse 17 states,

> "So all the generations from Abraham to David are fourteen generations; and from David until the carrying away into Babylon are fourteen generations; and from the carrying away into Babylon unto Christ are fourteen generations."

So, if Abraham was of the Black race, as proved, and David descended from him, and Jesus descended from David (and all the prophets, priests, kings and common people in-between), that would automatically make Jesus, too, of the Black race. He is recorded as having said in Revelation 22:16, "I am the root and the offspring of David," which harmonizes perfectly with the genealogy in Matthew chapter 1. Jesus had a Canaanite disciple, whose name was Simon – Simon the Canaanite (Matt. 10:4). The Canaanites were a Hamitic people. He had no Greek or Roman disciples.

This author places so great an emphasis on Jesus because of the fact that hundreds of millions who are of African ancestry among the nearly two billion Christians globally have been sold a "bill of goods" and are hoodwinked into believing a lie about the man they have been taught to pray to and worship. Our two previous books, THE DECEIVING OF THE BLACK RACE and A NON-CHRISTIAN'S RESPONSE TO CHRISTIANITY, are must-reads for our people – and for all peoples – for they set the record straight.

THEY ARE GETTING CLOSER AND CLOSER TO WHAT JESUS AND THE PROPHETS BEFORE HIM REALLY LOOKED LIKE!

Above is the **Discovery Channel's** version (April 9, 2001) of what Jesus looked like. Using the latest forensic and historical discoveries -- and a computer -- scientists have reconstructed the image of a first-century man who lived a life similar to and was around the age of Jesus.

A computer-generated image has been created to suggest what Jesus' face might have looked like, contrary to the fair-skinned and fine-featured image familiar since medieval times.

The new image was created by a forensic artist at the

university of Manchester using the 2,000-year-old skull of a Jewish man from Israel. Cues on hair and skin tone were taken from frescoes of Jewish faces painted in the third century.

The result is a dark-skinned, curly-haired man with a round robust face and a stout nose.

The idea of a darker Jesus is becoming more accepted by Catholics -- a dark-skinned Jesus was selected in 1999 for a special millennium-edition of the American Independent news weekly, the *National Catholic Reporter.*

Now is the time for all people of African ancestry to remove and discard all of the white Jesus pictures from their homes and from their Bibles. That's right, tear the pages out and trash them. If it is not expedient to tear them out, cover them over; it will be good for the psyche -- your mental state.

Does It Make Any Difference?

At our various book-signings and lectures, we meet so many brothers and sisters who insist on maintaining that *"it makes no difference of what race Abraham, Moses, David, Isaiah, Jeremiah, or Jesus were. Color doesn't matter with God."* If only we could convince the White race that this is true! Race and color certainly make a difference with them. Nearly everything that we must encounter today to survive is based on race, and the continual portrayal on TV of Europeans in their glory, with long, flowing hair and light skin being the standard of beauty, is to make non-Europeans -- especially African Americans -- feel inferior. In order to be accepted, many African Americans undergo make-overs in order to look more Caucasian.

It's All Temporary

Do you recall the scripture from the Book of the Prophet Isaiah which Dr. Martin Luther King, Jr., used to often quote?

It is quite relevant to this discussion, and is taken from Isaiah 40:3-5 --

> *"The voice of him that crieth in the wilderness, Prepare ye the way of the LORD, make straight in the desert a highway for our God. Every valley shall be exalted, and every mountain and hill shall be made low: and the crooked shall be made straight, and the rough places plain: And the glory of the LORD shall be revealed, and all flesh shall see it together: for the mouth of the LORD hath spoken it."*

The mention of "wilderness" and "desert" in the Biblical passage is not to be construed as geographical locations, but represent the spiritual entanglement of the hearts and minds of God's people, due to the polluted teachings of the oppressor. The wilderness and desert must be cleared so that the Most High may come through. And when He does, that will be the time when "Every valley [those in a low state] shall be exalted, and every mountain and hill [those ruling wickedly over God's Chosen] shall be made low: and the crooked shall be made straight, and the rough places plain." Crookedness and roughness have prevailed for many centuries now, but the Most High has promised that He will come and save us, and He will!

In every age the Almighty God has been our hope: He has always rescued us from enemies who sought to destoy us. That Divine Unseen Power forever keeps watch over the dim unknown. Keep faith in the Eternal One; for what the Most High God through men and women of faith has done once, He will do again! NEVER FORGET THAT *"DELIVERANCE IS PARTICIPATORY!"*

"Everything that has a beginning has an ending" -- <u>even</u> *our 400-year + dilemma!*

Chapter 13

WHY ARE WE THE MOST HATED RACE ON THE FACE OF THE EARTH?

ARE WE A THREAT because we are nearly 40 million strong in the U.S. alone? Is it because of our tenacity, and the determination of many of us to climb the ladder of success, despite the opposition? Is it due to the fact that other races see us as not unified, therefore they shun and mistreat us?

Their hatred toward us often spills over into their publications and enters into the public libraries, as has this most damning and racist article in the *ENCYCLOPEDIA JUDAICA* about the Black race of antiquity. Under its entry 'HAM', subheading 'In the Aggadah' (page 1215), the following appears:

> **IN THE AGGADAH.** Ham's descendant (Cush) is black skinned as a punishment for Ham's having had sexual intercourse in the ark. When Ham saw his drunken father exposed, he emasculated him, saying, "Adam had but two sons, and one slew the other; this man Noah has three sons, yet he desires to beget a fourth." Noah therefore cursed Canaan (Gen. 9:25), Ham's fourth son. According to another opinion, Ham committed sodomy with his father, and Noah cursed Canaan because Ham, together with his father

and two brothers, had previously been blessed by God. Another tradition attributes the curse to the fact that it was Canaan who castrated Noah. Ham was nevertheless the blame because he informed his brothers of their father's nakedness. Canaan was so wicked that his last will and testament to his children was: "Love one another, love robbery, love lewdness, hate your masters, and do not speak the truth." Ham was also punished in that his descendants, the Egyptians and Ethiopians, were taken captive and led into exile with their buttocks uncovered (Isa. 20:4). Ham was responsible for the ultimate transfer to Nimrod of the garments which God made for Adam and Eve before their expulsion from the Garden of Eden. From Adam and Eve these garments went to Enoch, and from him to Methuselah, and finally to Noah, who took them into the ark with him. When the inmates of the ark were about to leave their refuge, Ham stole the garments and kept them concealed for many years. Finally, he passed them on to his firstborn son, Cush, who eventually gave them to his son, Nimrod, when he reached his 20th year.

In other books authored and edited by White European Jews there is contained additional spurious information pertaining to Ham and his descendants. One example follows:

> "When God cursed Ham He turned him black, made his hair like wire, his eyes red like wine, his nose broad, and his lips thick like liver . . ."

It would be redundant for us to respond in full to all of the above unfounded statements, as we have already addressed in detail the power and greatnesss of the Hamitic people of past ages. In one of our previous books, in two chapters in particular, *The Bible: A Black History Book* and *Is the Black Race the Curse of Ham?*, we crush to the pit such lies that have been promulgated by our enemies. In their attempt to perpetuate these literary atrocities, they seek justification for our Enslavement and all the other abominable actions they have perpetrated upon us through the centuries. Legal steps should be taken to remove such books from the shelves of our libraries; racist literature has been banned from public access in the past.

Jeshua ben Yosef, whom the Greeks named *Jesus Christ*, warned his disciples (in John 16:2), saying,

> *"And they shall put you out of the synagogues: yea, the time cometh, that whosoever killeth you will think that he doeth God service."*

The same is true regarding our people today; many White racists feel and say that it is God's will that all who are not White -- Native Americans, African Americans, Hispanics, Asians, etc. -- should be annihilated.

Smith's Bible Dictionary of 1863 (no error, 1863) records that *"the descendants of Ham settled in Africa (Psa. 78:51, 105:23, 106:22), and also sent many branches into Asia (Canaanites)."* If Africa is the ancient home of the Black race, and the Black race is cursed of God, why is the African continent, of all the continents on earth, the richest in natural resources to this very day? And why is that portion of Asia -- formerly called *"the land of the Canaanites"* and *"Palestine"* (once totally inhabited by Black people and known today as the Middle East) -- metaphorically spoken of in Scripture as *"the land flowing with milk and honey,"* if the Black race is cursed of God?

Our dilemma, and the solution to it, are recorded throughout the pages of Holy Scripture. There is no one answer to the plethora of problems which beset us. Everything that we have tried so far has failed. For some reason, we think that the politicians, Black and White -- are going to free us. Some feel as though our salvation lies in the NAACP, in PUSH, in CORE, in the SCLC, or the Congress. Others are looking to renown Egyptological scholars and their messages of Afrocentricity for deliverance. But we stand firm on the declaration that our only perpetual Hope and our only perpetual Help is THE ALMIGHTY GOD AND HIS COMMAND-MENTS. The majority of the readers of this book may not believe the very things they see; but neither did all of ancient Israel believe the prophets whom the Most High sent to them. But for those who desire to know where to start, we offer the same promise which the Almighty made to His people 3,000 years ago, which has come down to us through the writings of the wise King Solomon. We do not contend that this is an end-all solution that will cure each of our economic, physical, academic, sociological and spiritual ills, but our experience has taught us that this is a good place to begin. We strongly suggest for your consideration II Chronicles 7:14:

> *"If My people, which are called by My name, shall humble themselves, and pray, and seek My face, and turn from their wicked ways; then will I hear from heaven, and will forgive their sin, and will heal their land."*

The Almighty and Most High Creator has not forsaken His people. It is the other way around -- **many people have forsaken the Almighty and His Laws for the Good Life.**

In addition to living in accordance with the above Scripture, do the following: 1. Educate yourselves and your children, and love the people of your race. 2. Read good, wholesome books; the mind and soul must also be fed. 3. Eat only the right foods -- no pork, less beef (really, no beef), more fish and good quality chicken. 4. Become more overall health-conscious. 5. No alcohol or tobacco. 6. Exercise often; walking briskly is good. 7. Lose weight, if necessary. 8. Drink plenty of water. 9. Eat plenty fresh fruits and vegetables. 10. Take a good multiple vitamin. 11. Strive to be happy! 12. Have high self esteem, but not to the point of being proud or arrogant. *"If you always do what you've always done, you'll always get what you've always got."*

And, One Final Note: We as a race of people must take greater interest in our Youth, by precept and example. Face it, we are in America. If we desire ourselves and our children to excel, there are certain standards which must be met. Everyone is not going to obtain a college degree, but everyone should learn, and learn well, a marketable skill in the form of a trade or profession that will demand a decent wage. It is imperative that we have a good command of the English language.

These ten simple rules, if followed, will take you a long way in life:

1. Bank some money out of every pay check; 10% is recommended.
2. Do not spend money unnecessarily, but at the same time don't be a free-loader or a tight wad.
3. Don't be noisy on the streets.
4. Give your employer an honest day's work, regardless of his race.
5. Do not steal from your employer.
6. Keep yourselves and children clean.
7. Make no trouble for law enforcement officers.
8. Do not disrespect your parents. Listen to the advice of the older generation; weigh it, and use what's useable.
9. Don't follow the crowd; do what you know is right.
10. Manners will carry you further than money.

"Miss, you'll have to move to the back of the bus, and give this man your seat." She didn't.

"Never move from that which is right!"

---

*"Go **up**, Moses; you've been down long enough!"*

Chapter 14

MORE LIGHT ON YESHUA BEN YOSEF
(Jesus of Nazareth)

(The following are <u>excerpts</u> from a creditable Atlas entitled FORTY CENTURIES, *and gives a fresh look at the Jesus of history. It tells, among other things, how the Romans were totally responsible for his crucifixion, and not the Jews, as the New Testament account depicts. (It is necessary to point out here, as we have done so often in the past, that Jesus' real name was not "Jesus," but "Yeshua ben Yosef," which by interpretation is "Jesus, son of Joseph." The Greeks named him Jesus.)*

For the Romans alive about A.D. 30, the life and death of Jesus was of no significance whatsoever. In the context of Roman history, Jesus was just another rebellious troublemaker. After the revolt of Spartacus thousands of slaves had been crucified in the same way as Jesus. His death was merely one more item in the list of repressions that Rome found necessary to carry out in order to consolidate her power. And yet in the end the religion <u>which is said</u> to have been founded by Jesus would take over the Roman Empire itself, and eventually make its way all over the world. The consequences for the subsequent history of civilization were incalculable.

THE CHRISTIAN GOSPELS purport to give factual accounts of the life of Jesus; but these writings are based on the <u>assump-</u>

tion that Jesus was not just a man, but that he was the Son of God, sent by God into the world to save mankind. This assumption involved some very complex theology; it had nothing to do with historical fact.

Ironically, the most certain fact that we know about Jesus is that he was crucified by the Romans for sedition against their government in Judaea. The Roman governor who ordered his execution was Pontius Pilate, who held the office of Governor of Judaea from A.D. 26 to 36. We can be certain of this one fact because the Roman execution of Jesus is recorded not only by the Roman historian Tacitus, but also by the authors of the four gospels, who might have wished to suppress such damaging evidence. That Jesus had been crucified for sedition was indeed an embarrassing fact. For Jesus' followers it meant that their master had been regarded as a rebel against Rome, and that they were likely to be incriminated as well.

His early followers would probably have preferred to keep quiet about the execution of Jesus, but the fact was too well known to conceal. Instead, they attempted to show that Jesus was really innocent of sedition. A large part of each of the four Gospels is devoted to the trial and crucifixion of Jesus. The Gospel of Mark, earliest of the four, sets the theme for the others by endeavoring to show that the death of Jesus had been plotted by Jewish leaders who hated him. These leaders, Mark points out, condemned Jesus to death for blasphemy in their own court, the Sanhedrin; but they lacked the authority to execute him. Consequently, they handed Jesus over to Pilate, charging him with sedition against Rome. . . .

The most certain fact we know about Jesus thus entails a problem: Christian evidence admits that Jesus was executed for sedition against Rome; but it also maintains that he was innocent. Can this claim be accepted? The question is basic to all understanding of Jesus as a historical person. . . .

Roman rule was an affront to the Jews' religion since they fervently believed they were the Elect People of their god Yahweh and should not be subject to a heathen lord. . . . Many Jews, in fact, refused to submit to Rome and died as martyrs for Israel's freedom. The usual Roman penalty for rebellion was crucifixion. Hence the problem: did Jesus also die as a martyr for Israel's freedom? Or was he obedient to Rome, as the Gospels make out, and was his crucifixion due to the Jewish leaders?

The Gospel accounts of the trial of Jesus reveal a strong apologetic motivation. The early Christian authors were obviously concerned with transferring the responsibility for the crucifixion of Jesus from the Romans to the Jews. . . .

Mark's attempt to turn Pilate into a witness to the innocence of Jesus and make the Jews solely responsible for his death breaks down under critical analysis. This is also the case when the accounts of the trial of Jesus in the other Gospels are examined. We must conclude, therefore, that the Romans crucified Jesus as a rebel because they deemed him to be one. . . .

The crucifixion of Jesus as a rebel by the Romans was not an extraordinary event in the light of contemporary Jewish history. Thousands of other Jews similarly perished, either as leaders or supporters of revolt. But from this point onwards Christian tradition makes even more problematic the search for historical fact about Jesus. It was the usual practice for the bodies of executed criminals to be buried in a common grave. According to the Gospels, this did not happen to the body of Jesus. Instead, a disciple named Joseph of Arimathaea obtained the body from Pilate and buried it in a rock-hewn tomb of his own. Three days later, the tomb was found to be empty. Subsequently a series of visions, in which the crucified Jesus appeared to various disciples, convinced his followers that Jesus had risen from the dead. The visions were, significantly, limited to the disciples of Jesus; no one outside their fellowship is recorded to have had a similar experience. According to Christian tradition, these appearances of the Risen Jesus continued for forty days.

It is difficult to evaluate these traditions of the Resurrection of Jesus. Although the physical reality of the Risen Jesus is stressed, it is never asserted that he resumed his life on earth; instead he is said to have ascended to heaven. But, whatever the truth of the traditions about the Risen Jesus, there can be no doubt that from the disciples' faith in it, Christianity was born.

When the original disciples of Jesus became convinced that he had risen from the dead, their faith in his Messiahship revived. But, in light of their new conviction, they had to adjust their own Jewish ideas. According to contemporary belief, the Messiah would overthrow the nation's oppressors and "restore the kingdom of Israel." But Jesus had been executed by Israel's oppressors: how could he, then, be the Messiah? The disciples soon found a solution in Holy Scripture. The prophet Isaiah had spoken about a Suffering Servant of Yahweh, and the disciples applied this prophecy to Jesus. Because of Israel's sins, Jesus had died as a martyr; but God had raised him up. He would soon return, with supernatural power, to fulfill his Messianic role and redeem Israel.

The transformation of Christianity from a Jewish Messianic sect into a universal salvation-religion, centered on Jesus, was due to Paul of Tarsus. Paul had not been an original disciple of Jesus. In fact, he had at first fiercely rejected Jewish Christianity because it preached a "crucified Messiah" -- a scandalous thing to a pious Jew -- and helped persecute members of the movement.

Paul's new conception of Jesus drew its inspiration from Hellenistic (Greek) ideas rather than from Judaism. It was a very esoteric doctrine but one that Greco-Roman society of that time could understand and appreciate. **Jesus was presented by Paul as a savior-god, who had died and risen again.** Through the sacrament of baptism, Christians were ritually identified with Jesus in his death and resurrection. In consequence, they were reborn to a new risen life *in Christos*. Paul's version of Christianity survived and set the pattern for the entire faith.

Christianity moved mainly northwestwards, through Syria and Asia Minor, to Greece and Italy. . . . Freed from its Jewish cradle, Christianity quickly adapted itself to the spiritual needs of Greco-Roman society and eventually even survived the downfall of the Roman Empire in the West. The subsequent conversion of the barbarian peoples, who were to form the new nations of Europe, gave the Christian Church immense influence and power. The civilization of medieval Europe was, indeed, essentially the product of Christianity, and the later predominance and diffusion of the European peoples throughout the world made Christianity a cultural force of universal influence. . . .

By the sixth century, Christians regarded the birth of Jesus as so significant a turning point in world history that they reckoned time from it -- *Anno Domini* (A.D.), the "years of the Lord," that continue to designate our present era.

THE END.

Chapter 15

Tidbits on Slavery, and What Abraham Lincoln Had to Say

TODAY'S BLACKS who call in on national radio and TV talk shows declaring, "We should forget about Slavery; that was over 100 years ago," are really to be pitied, as they do not have a clue as to Slavery's present-day effects.

The following are excerpts from *AFRO USA: A REFERENCE WORK ON THE BLACK EXPERIENCE*. Copyrighted in 1971, this work has more than 1,100 pages and was compiled and edited by eminent scholars:

"The slave trade in the western hemisphere began formally in 1517, the year the Spanish resolved to encourage immigration to Latin America by allowing each Spanish settler a quota of 12 Negro slaves."

"The voyage from Africa to the Caribbean Sea, known as the 'Middle Passage,' was filled with misery and degradation for the slave. He slept in overcrowded quarters, was often mercilessly beaten, and was subject to disease and malnutrition. The mere fact that he survived the ordeal made him a valuable commodity. . . ."

"Although the African slave trade was technically discontinued in 1808 (it is estimated that, from that date until 1860, no less than 250,000 slaves were in fact imported, the ban notwithstanding), nothing prevented slaves from being bred and battered within various territories of the United

States proper. Virginia, for example, earned the title of the 'Negro-raising state' by virtue of its being able to export over 6,000 slaves annually to such centers of trade as Baltimore, Washington, DC, Charleston, Montgomery, Memphis, and New Orleans."

Abraham Lincoln on Slavery

"Slavery" shared the spotlight with the "Preservation of the Union" as the paramount issues of the Civil War. It can be said that both questions had to be resolved simultaneously, or not at all. Abraham Lincoln, elected to the presidency as a racial moderate in 1860, came to power knowing full well that slavery was wrong, but arguing nonetheless that the federal government had no right to prohibit slavery in the South. He even went so far as to say the following:

"If I could save the Union without freeing any slave, I would do it; if I could save it by freeing all the slaves, I would do it; and if I could save it by freeing some and leaving others alone, I would also do that. What I do about slavery and the colored race, I do because I believe it helps save the Union. . . ."

For those who contend that "we should forget about Slavery," this quotation from *AFRO USA* is for you:

"For our purposes, Slavery as a <u>legal</u> concept ended in the year 1865, <u>although its repercussions continue to plague our race down to our very own time.</u>"

2 OF SEVERAL ARGUMENTS FOR SLAVERY

1. **Necessity.** *"Agricultural and industrial surpluses could not be produced, nor could public works projects or cultural monuments be undertaken, without the use of*

slave labor. Slavery was needed to create wealth and grandeur."

2. **Profit.** *"Slavery was profitable to those engaged in the trade. Their well-being was not isolated, but contributed instead to the good fortune of others."*

The Montgomery Bus Boycott
(1955-1956)

Excerpts

The Montgomery bus boycott was a 382-day-long protest movement in which "direct action" was effectively used for the first time in the South with the primary objective of dramatizing the effects of racial discrimination on a Black community – in this case, one in Alabama. . . .

The arrest of Mrs. Rosa Parks was a "last straw" to the Black community which, within 24 hours, had decided to call a bus boycott, and keep some 17,000 Blacks from riding this public conveyance indefinitely. The task of organizing the boycott fell to Dr. Martin Luther King, Jr., then an unheralded 27-year-old clergyman with little experience in the techniques of mass protest. Dr. King coordinated the activities of the boycotters by forming the Montgomery Improvement Association (MIA). . . .

The bus boycott had numerous concrete results, and several important psychological ones. For one thing, it established Dr. King as a new voice in the ranks of Black leadership; **for another, it opened the eyes of the urban Black to the strength he could command when united behind a coordinated program for the assertion of his rights as a citizen.** What happened in Montgomery proved to be symptomatic of what was soon to follow in several other cities across the South.

Blacks and whites board a public transit bus in Montgomery after the Supreme Court ruling against Alabama's "Jim Crow" laws.

About the Authors

STEVEN S. JACOBS

JACOBS IS A EUROPEAN JEW and a life-long resident of Philadelphia, PA. He is a graduate of Gratz College in Philadelphia where he did extensive studies in African History and African American History. Jacobs is fluent in the Hebrew language and has spent untold years in the study and teaching of Torah. He has personally traveled to the Middle East and witnessed first-hand many of the lands and people mentioned in his book. His research is exhaustive.

If you really desire to be enlightened from antiquity to the present on the subject of Black Hebrews, this book, *"The Hebrew Heritage of Black Africa,"* is the book to read!

MOSES FARRAR

FARRAR IS AN ORDAINED Hebrew Israelite Elder. A native of Richmond, VA, he spent 25 years in Philadelphia, PA, and 19 years in Brooklyn, NY, where he presently resides. Farrar, a Biblical historian and researcher, is the author of three other books, *"The Deceiving of the Black Race,"* *"A Non-Christian's Response To Christianity,"* and *"What Will It Take To Wake Us Up?"* He has been minister-in-charge of Israelite congregations in four different cities, serving for a total of 25 years, and is listed in the 2000-2004 editions of *"Who's Who Among African Americans."*

As author of Part II of this book, he offers interesting reading and plenty of food for thought. Elder Farrar also conducts historical and spiritual seminars, and is a lecturer, teacher and vocalist.

- NOTES -

Made in the USA
Lexington, KY
05 January 2017